Follow

Your

Heart

Susanna Tamaro

Translated from the Italian by John Cullen

Delta
Trade Paperbacks

A Delta Book
Published by
Dell Publishing
a division of
Bantam Doubleday Dell Publishing Group, Inc.
1540 Broadway
New York, New York 10036

ISBN: 0-385-31657-7

Reprinted by arrangement with Doubleday

Manufactured in the United States of America
Published simultaneously in Canada

September 1996

20 19 18 17 16 15 14 13

BVG

To Pietro

O Shiva, what is your reality?
What is this universe so full of wonder?
What forms the seed?
What is the hub of the universal wheel?
What is this life beyond the form that pervades
  the forms?
How can we enter fully into it, above space
  and time, names and features?
Clarify my doubts!

> —From a sacred text of Kashmiri
> Shiva-worship

Follow Your Heart

Opicina,
November 17, 1992

YOU'VE BEEN GONE for two months, and for two months I haven't heard anything from you, except for the postcard you sent to let me know you were still alive. This morning, in the garden, I stood in front of your rose for a long time. Even though we're well into fall, it's still bright red, standing out solitary and arrogant while the other plants are brown and dead. Do you remember when we planted it? You were ten years old, and you had just finished reading *The Little Prince,* a present from me for passing fifth grade. You loved that story. Of all the characters, your favorites were the rose and the fox; you didn't like the baobab tree, the snake, the aviator, or any of the empty, conceited men sitting on their minuscule planets. So one morning, while we were having breakfast, you said, "I want a rose." When I objected that we already had lots of roses, you said, "I want one that's all mine, I want to take care of it and make it grow tall." Naturally, along with the rose, you also wanted a fox. With a child's cunning you had put the simple request before the almost-impossible one. How could I refuse you a fox when I had already agreed to a rose? We discussed this point for a long time, and at last we compromised on a dog.

The night before we went to pick it up you didn't sleep a wink. Every half hour you knocked on my door and said, "I can't sleep." By seven the next morning, you'd already washed, dressed, and had breakfast, and you were sitting in an armchair with your overcoat on, waiting for me. At eight-thirty we were at the entrance to the kennels, which were still closed. You kept peering through the bars and asking me, "How will I know which one's mine?" There was so much anxiety in your voice. I tried to reassure you. Don't worry, I said, remember how the Little Prince tamed the fox.

We went back to the kennels three days in a row. There were more than two hundred dogs in there, and you wanted to see them all. You stopped in front of every cage and stood there without moving, looking distracted and indifferent, while the dogs flung themselves against the wire mesh and barked and jumped around and tried to tear the links apart with their paws. The woman who ran the place was with us. She thought you were an ordinary little girl, so she kept on trying to interest you in the best-looking dogs. "Look at that cocker spaniel," she would say, or "How do you like that collie?" The only reply you gave was a sort of grunt, and you continued on without listening to her.

On the third day of this ordeal we came upon Buck. He was in the back, in one of the pens where they kept the convalescing dogs. When we got there, instead of running to greet us with all the others, he remained sitting where he was, not even raising his head. "That one!" you cried, pointing at him. "I want *that* dog." Do you remember the astonished look on the woman's face? She just couldn't understand how you could want to own that pitiful mongrel. Of course she couldn't. Buck looked as though every canine race in the world had gone into the making of his little body, with his wolf's head, his soft, droopy hunting dog's ears, his long dachshund's paws, his fluffy Pomeranian's tail, his black-and-red Doberman's coat. When we went into the office to sign the papers, the girl who worked there told us his story. Someone had thrown him out of a moving car at the beginning of the summer. He'd been so severely hurt that one of his hind legs hung down useless.

Buck's right here by my side. Every now and then, while I write, he sighs and touches my leg with the tip of his nose. His muzzle and ears have become almost white, and for some time now he's had that film over his eyes that all old dogs get. It touches me to look at him. It's as though a part of you were here beside me, the part I love the most, the part that considered two hundred dogs in that shelter so many years ago and then picked out the saddest, ugliest one of all.

In my solitary wanderings around the house during these past months, the years of misunderstanding and bad feeling when we lived together have disappeared. The memories that surround me are memories of you as a child, so ingenuous and vulnerable and confused. It's her I'm writing to, to that child, not to the arrogant, defensive person of later years. The rose gave me the idea. When I walked past it this morning, it seemed to say, "Take out some paper and write her a letter." I know that one of the agreements we made when you left was that we wouldn't write, and I'm sticking to it, but reluctantly. These lines will never make their way to you in America. If I'm not here when you come back, they'll be here waiting for you. Why do I say this? Because less than a month ago, for the first time in my life, I was seriously ill. And so now I know that among all the other possibilities, there's also this one: that in six or seven months I may not be here anymore to open the door for you and put my arms around you. Some time ago a friend was telling me that when sickness comes to people who have always been healthy, it strikes them suddenly and violently. That's just what happened to me: one morning, while I was watering the rose, someone suddenly turned off the lights. If Mrs. Razman hadn't seen me through the fence between our gardens, you'd almost certainly be an orphan right now. Orphan? Is that what you call someone whose grandmother has died? I'm not really sure. Maybe grandparents aren't considered important enough to require a special term for being without them. You don't become an orphan or a widow when you lose your grandparents. It seems natural for them to get left along the way, absentmindedly, like forgotten umbrellas.

When I woke up in the hospital I didn't remember anything at all. While my eyes were still closed I had the feeling I had grown two long, thin whiskers, like a cat's. But as soon as I opened them I realized there were two little plastic tubes that started inside my nostrils and ran along my lips. I was surrounded by strange machines. After a few days I was transferred to a regular room where

November 17, 1992

there were already two other patients. One afternoon Mr. and Mrs. Razman came to see me. He told me, "That dog of yours was barking like mad. He's the reason you're still alive."

After I started to get back on my feet, I had a visit from a young doctor who had been in to check on me several times before. He took a chair and sat next to my bed. "Since you don't have any relatives to take care of you and make decisions for you," he said, "I have to talk to you directly. I'll be frank." So he talked to me, and while he talked, I was watching him more than listening to him. He had thin lips, and as you know I've never liked thin-lipped people. According to him, I was in such bad shape I couldn't go back home. He told me the names of two or three old folks' homes with nursing facilities where I could go and live. He must have read the expression on my face, because he added right away, "Don't think those homes are what they used to be. Everything's changed nowadays—the rooms are bright and sunny, and there are big gardens to walk in all around." I said to him, "Doctor, do you know anything about the Eskimos?" "Of course I do," he said as he stood up. "Well, the thing is, I want to die the way they do," I said, and since he didn't seem to understand, I went on. "I'd rather die facedown among the zucchini in my vegetable garden than live an extra year stuck to a bed in a whitewashed room." By then he was already at the door, but before he disappeared he gave me a nasty smile. "Lots of people say that sort of thing," he said. "Then at the last minute they come running back here, desperate to be looked after and trembling like leaves."

Three days later I signed a ridiculous statement in which I declared that if I should die the responsibility would be mine and mine alone. I handed this thing over to a young nurse with a tiny head and two enormous gold earrings, gathered up my little belongings into a plastic bag, and headed for the taxi stand.

As soon as Buck saw me at the gate, he started running around in circles like a crazy thing; then, just to remove any doubts I may have had about the true extent of his felicity, he demolished two or three flowerbeds, barking all the while. For once, I didn't have the heart to scold him. When he came up to me with his nose covered with dirt, I said to him, "See, old boy? We're together again," and I scratched the back of his ears.

In the days that followed I did little or nothing. Since my incident, the left side of my body doesn't obey my commands the way it used to. My left hand especially has become very slow. I hate to let it get the best of me, so I'm forcing myself to use it more than my right one. I've tied a pink bow to my wrist, so that every time I have to reach for

November 17, 1992

something I remember to use my left hand instead of my right. As long as your body's in good working order, you don't realize what a great enemy it can be; and if your will to struggle against it weakens for so much as an instant, you're lost.

In any case, it looks as though my autonomy is shrinking, so I've given Walter's wife a set of keys. She drops in for a visit every day and brings me whatever I need.

As I drift about the house and garden, the thought of you has grown so insistent that it's a genuine obsession. Several times I've gone so far as to pick up the telephone to send you a telegram, but every time the operator came on the line I changed my mind. In the evening, sitting in my armchair—with the void in front of me and silence all around—I would ask myself what would be the best thing to do. Best for you, naturally, not for me. For me, of course it would be much nicer to have you beside me when I go. If I had told you about my illness, I'm sure you would have interrupted your stay in America and rushed home. And then? And then, who knows, I might live for another three or four years, maybe confined to a wheelchair, maybe even with my mind gone, and you would do your duty and look after me. You'd do it with dedication, but as time passed that dedication would transform itself into anger and resentment. Resentment because the years would have passed and you'd have wasted your youth; because my love, with a sort of boomerang effect, would have forced your life into a blind alley. Or so the voice inside me that didn't want to telephone you said. But as soon as I decided that it was right, another voice chimed in, arguing the opposite. What would happen to you, I wondered, if you opened the door and found an empty house, uninhabited for a long time, instead of finding Buck and me celebrating your homecoming? Is there anything more terrible than an incomplete return? If a telegram had reached you over there with the news of my death, wouldn't you have felt that it was a sort of betrayal? A dirty trick? You've been quite rude to me in recent months, so I punish you by going away without warning. That wouldn't have been a boomerang, but an abyss; I don't think anyone could survive such a thing. Imagine: whatever you wanted to say to someone you loved has to stay inside you forever; she's buried in her grave, you can't look into her eyes anymore, can't embrace her, can't ever say the things to her that you hadn't yet said.

The days were slipping by and I wasn't reaching any kind of decision. Then, this morning, the rose prompted me. Write her a letter, a little record of your days for her to keep after you're gone. And so here I am in the kitchen staring at one of your old exercise books and chewing my pen like a child

November 17, 1992

having trouble with her homework. Writing my testament? Not exactly; I'd rather think of it as something that will stay with you through the years, something you can read whenever you feel you need me close to you. Don't worry, I don't intend to preach or try to make you sad, I just want to chat with you, heart-to-heart, the way we used to do before the last few years estranged us. Now that I've lived so long and left so many people behind, I know that the absence of the dead doesn't weigh on us so heavily as the words that were left unsaid between us when they died.

You see, I found myself having to be your mother when I was already up in years, at an age when one is usually just a grandmother. There were many advantages to this. Advantages for you, because a grandma-mother is always more attentive and good-natured than a mother-mother, and advantages for me, because instead of growing senile like other ladies my age with their canasta parties and afternoon teas, I was dragged by force back into the mainstream of life. Somewhere along the line, however, something broke. It wasn't my fault, and it wasn't yours. Blame it on the laws of nature.

Childhood and old age resemble one another. In both cases, for different reasons, we're more or less defenseless, we can't yet—or can't any longer—play an active part in life, and so our responses are natural and uncalculated. Adolescence is the period when an invisible shell begins to form around our body, and it continues to thicken throughout our adult life. Its growth process is a little like a pearl's; the bigger and deeper the wound, the stronger the protective layer that grows around it. Then, however, with the passage of time, like a dress that's been worn too often, the stress points begin to weaken, the weave starts to show, a sudden movement rips it open. At first you don't notice anything, you're convinced that your armor is completely intact, then one day something insignificant happens and all at once you find yourself crying like a baby.

So when I say that a natural rift opened up between us, that's just what I mean. When your shell was beginning to form, mine was already in shreds. You couldn't stand my tears, and I couldn't stand your sudden callousness. Although I was prepared for your character to change with adolescence, once the change took place it was hard for me to bear. Suddenly there was a new person in front of me, and I had no idea what to do with her. At night, when I gathered my thoughts, I'd be glad for what was happening to you. I'd tell myself that no one who gets through adolescence unscathed can ever become a full-fledged adult. But the next morning, when you slammed the first door in my face, it was too depressing, it made me

November 17, 1992

want to cry. I just couldn't find enough energy to stand up to you. If you ever get to be eighty years old, you'll understand that at that age you feel like a leaf at the end of September. There's less daylight, and little by little the tree's drawing back into itself everything that can nourish it. Nitrogen, chlorophyll, and proteins get sucked back into the trunk, greenness goes away, elasticity too. You're still hanging on up there, but clearly it's just a matter of time. One by one the leaves around you drop, you watch them fall, you live terrified that the wind might rise. For me the wind was you, your combative adolescent vitality. Didn't you ever notice, sweetheart? We lived on the same tree, but in altogether different seasons.

I'm thinking about the day you left. We sure were nervous, weren't we? You refused to let me go with you to the airport, and every time I reminded you to pack something, your reply was, "I'm going to America, not the desert." When you got to the door, I called out to you in my hatefully shrill voice, "Take care of yourself." Without even turning around, you said, "Take care of Buck and the rose."

You know, at the time I was disappointed by those parting words. Sentimental old woman that I am, I was expecting something different, something more banal, such as a kiss or a few terms of endearment. Only that night, when I couldn't sleep and was wandering around the empty house in my robe, did I realize that taking care of Buck and the rose meant taking care of the part of you that's still living with me, the happy part. And I also realized why you gave me such a curt command; you weren't being insensitive, you were very tense and on the verge of tears. It's the shell I was talking about before—yours is so tight you can hardly breathe. Remember what I kept telling you during those last months? Unshed tears leave a deposit on your heart. Eventually they form a crust around it and paralyze it, the way mineral deposits paralyze a washing machine.

I know, my homely metaphors fail to amuse you. You may as well resign yourself—we all draw inspiration from the world we know best.

I must leave you for now. Buck is sighing and staring at me with imploring eyes. He's a study in the rhythms of nature. Whatever the season, he can tell mealtime with the precision of a Swiss watch.

November 17, 1992

November 18

IT RAINED really hard last night. The pounding against the shutters was so loud it woke me up several times. When I opened my eyes this morning the weather still looked bad, so I stayed snuggled up under the covers for a good while. Things certainly change as the years go by! At your age I was like a dormouse, if nobody disturbed me I could sleep until lunchtime. Now, on the other hand, I'm always awake before dawn, and so the days go on and on interminably. Pretty cruel, don't you think? Besides, the morning hours are the very worst, there aren't any distractions, you're just there and you know your thoughts can only go

24

backward. An old person's thoughts have no future; they're sad, for the most part, or melancholy at best. I've often tried to figure out this quirk of nature. The other day I saw a TV documentary that made me think. The subject was animals' dreams. All creatures in the animal hierarchy, from birds on up, dream a lot. Titmice and pigeons dream, so do rabbits and squirrels, so do dogs and the cows lying in the fields. They all dream, but not all in the same way. Animals that are basically prey have short dreams, more like apparitions than real dreams. In contrast, predators' dreams are long and complicated. The narrator said, "Oneiric activity is a way of organizing survival strategies. Hunters must incessantly work out new methods of getting food for themselves, while those that are hunted—grass-eaters whose food is generally right there in front of them—have to think about only one thing: the fastest way to escape."

So the sleeping antelope sees the open savannah stretching out in front of him, but the lion dreams continual variations on the theme of what he'll have to do before he can succeed in eating the antelope. I thought that this must mean that you're a carnivore when you're young and a herbivore when you're old. Because old folks, aside from not sleeping very much, don't dream, or if they do have dreams maybe they forget them. Children and young people dream a lot more, and their dreams are vivid enough to determine their mood for an entire day. Do you remember how you started crying as soon as you woke up those last few months? You'd be sitting there with your coffee cup in front of you and the tears silently rolling down your cheeks. If I asked you why you were crying, you'd look even more dejected and say, "I don't know." At your age there are so many things that you have to get straight in your mind, you've got lots of projects and you're insecure about all of them. Your unconscious doesn't have any order or clear logic; it takes the leftover scraps from every day, no matter how swollen or distorted they may be, and scrambles them together with a mixture of your highest aspirations and your basic bodily needs. So someone who's hungry dreams that he's sitting at a table and can't eat, someone who's cold dreams he's at the North Pole without an overcoat, someone who's been insulted becomes a bloodthirsty warrior.

What kinds of dreams are you having over there among the cactus and the cowboys? I'd love to know. Do I show up every now and then, maybe dressed as a squaw? Does Buck appear too, disguised as a coyote? Are you homesick? Do you think about us?

You know, yesterday evening, while I was in my armchair reading, I suddenly heard a rhythmic noise in the room. I looked up and saw that Buck was sleeping and beating the floor with his tail. The expression on his face was so blissful I'm sure he was dreaming about you. Maybe you had just come back and he was celebrating, or maybe he was remembering some particularly fine walk you went on together. Dogs are so attuned to human emotions, they've lived with us for so long, starting way back in the mists of time, that we've practically become equals. That's why so many people detest dogs. They see too many aspects of themselves reflected in that tender, slavish doggy gaze, aspects they'd rather not know about. Buck often dreams about you these days. I haven't been able to, or maybe I have and can't remember.

When I was little, one of my father's sisters, a recent widow, lived with us for a while. She was a passionate spiritualist, and whenever we were out of my parents' sight, hiding in some dark corner, she'd teach me things about the extraordinary powers of the mind. "If you want to contact someone who's far away," she'd say, "you must clasp his photograph in your hand, step three paces in the form of a cross, and then say, 'It's me, here I am.' " That way, according to her, I could have telepathic communication with the person of my choice.

Before I started writing this afternoon, that's just what I did. It was about five o'clock, it must have been morning where you are. Did you see me? Or hear me? I spotted you in one of those bars filled with lights and colored tiles and people eating cooked meat sandwiches. There was a big, colorful crowd, but I picked you out at once because you were wearing the last sweater I knitted for you, the one with the red and blue stags. But everything went by so fast, and the images were so excessively like the ones I see in television movies, that I didn't have time to catch the expression in your eyes. Are you happy? More than anything else, that's what I care about.

Do you remember how many discussions we had about whether I should pay for your studies abroad? You insisted that this long sojourn was an absolute necessity for you, that your mind couldn't grow unless you got away from the suffocating atmosphere you were raised in. You had just finished high school, and you were fumbling around in total darkness as to what you wanted to do when you grew up. As a little girl you had so many passionate interests: you wanted to be a veterinarian, an explorer, a doctor caring for poor children. All these ambitions vanished without a trace. The initial openness you had shown toward others closed more and more narrowly as time passed; it didn't take very long for all your philanthropic or compassionate impulses to become cynicism, alienation, obsession with your own unhappy fate. If we happened to see some particularly cruel news story on television, you'd make fun of me for being shocked or sympathetic. "How can that surprise you at your age?" you'd say. "Haven't you figured it out yet? Natural selection rules the world!"

At first, remarks like this took my breath away, I seemed to have my very own monster sitting right there beside me. I'd look at you out of the corner of my eye and wonder where you came from, was this what my example had taught you. I never answered you, though, because I sensed that the time for dialogue was over, whatever I might say would only lead to a fight. For one thing, I was afraid of my own frailty, afraid to waste my strength, and for another I felt that an open confrontation was just what you were looking for and that others would follow on its heels, one after another, each more violent than the last. I could feel the energy seething behind your words, an arrogant energy barely restrained and ready to explode; I smoothed things over, feigned indifference to your attacks, and you were forced to look for other outlets.

That was when you threatened to go away, to disappear from my life without a trace. Maybe you were expecting me to act like a desperate old woman and humbly beg you to stay. When I told you your leaving was a good idea, you started wavering, you seemed like a snake with raised head and open jaws, ready to strike, and suddenly there's nothing for him to sink his fangs into. Then you began negotiating, you offered various hazy proposals, until finally one day at coffee you announced to me in a new, confident tone, "I'm going to America."

I greeted this decision like the others, with friendly interest. I didn't want my approval to propel you into hasty decisions you weren't perfectly sure about. In the following weeks you continued talking about the idea of going to America. "If I spend a year there," you kept repeating, "at least I'll learn another language and I won't be wasting time." I irritated you vastly when I pointed out that there was nothing wrong with wasting time, but your irritation went over the top when I declared that life isn't a race, it's a target-shoot: saving time doesn't count, what's important is the ability to hit the center. You sent our two cups flying off the table with a sweep of your arm, and then you burst into tears. "You're stupid," you said, hiding your face in your hands. "You're stupid. Don't you understand that's just what I want?" For weeks we'd been like two soldiers who'd buried a mine in a field and were being really careful not to step on it. We knew where it was and what it was and we were walking far apart, pretending the thing we feared was something else. When it finally blew up and you were sobbing, telling me you don't understand anything, you'll never understand anything, I had to make an enormous effort to hide my complete bewilderment. Your mother, the way she conceived you, her death—I've never spoken to you about any of that, and my silence has led you to believe that those things didn't affect me, that they weren't very important. But your mother was my daughter, maybe you don't take that fact into consideration. Or maybe you do, but instead of talking about it you brood over it. Otherwise I can't explain the way you look at me sometimes or the hateful things you say. You don't remember anything about her, just the empty place where she was supposed to be; you were still too young the day she died. But I have thirty-three years' worth of memories, thirty-three years plus the nine months I carried her in my womb.

How could you think I was indifferent to all this?

Shyness and a good deal of selfishness were the reasons why I never brought up the subject before. I shied away from talking about your mother because that would inevitably lead to talking about myself and my misdeeds, both real and alleged; and I was selfish because I hoped that my love would be great enough to cover the loss of hers, great enough to prevent you from missing her and asking me, "Who was my mother, why did she die?"

As long as you were a child, we were happy together. Your little heart was full of joy, but your joy wasn't ever cheap or superficial. The shadow of serious thought was always lying in wait for it, you could pass from laughter to silence with surprising ease. "What is it, what are you thinking about?" I'd ask, and you'd reply, as though you were talking about your afternoon snack, "I'm wondering whether the sky ends or goes on forever." I was proud that you were like that, your sensitivity was like mine, I didn't feel there were any gaps between us: we were friends and partners. I had the delusion—I fostered the delusion—that things would stay like this forever. But unfortunately we're not suspended in soap bubbles, merrily drifting through the air; there's a before and an after in our lives, and this before and after catches us in a trap, it settles down around us like a net. It's said that the sins of the fathers fall upon the children. This is true, absolutely true, the fathers' sins do fall upon the children, the grandfathers' sins on the grandchildren, the great-grandfathers' sins on the great-grandchildren. Some truths are liberating, others are terrifying: this one falls into the second category. Where does the chain of guilt start? With Cain? Do we have to go back that far? Is there something behind all this? I read once in a book of Indian philosophy that fate is inevitable and free will is just an illusion. After I read this a feeling of great peace came over me. But the very next day, a few pages further on, I found the assertion that fate is nothing but the result of our past actions, that we forge our destiny with our own hands. So I was back where I started. Where's the key to all this? I wondered. Which thread unwinds the skein? And is it a thread, or something stronger? Can we cut it or break it, or does it bind us forever?

Well, I'll do some breaking right here, because my head's not what it used to be. Sure, the ideas are still there, my way of thinking hasn't changed, but I can't make a sustained effort anymore. I'm tired now, my head's spinning the way it used to when I tried to read philosophy books as a girl. Being, nonbeing, immanence—after a few pages I had that dazed feeling you get when you ride a bus on mountain roads. I'm leaving you for now. I think I'll go into the living room and stupefy myself in front of that lovable detestable little box.

November 18

November 20

HERE WE ARE again, it's the third day of our meeting. Or rather the fourth day and the third meeting. I was so tired yesterday I couldn't even manage to read, let alone write. Since I felt restless and didn't know what to do with myself, I spent the whole day wandering about the house and garden. The air was pretty mild, and during the warmest part of the day I sat on the bench by the forsythia. All around me the lawn and the flower-beds were in utter disorder. As I looked at them I recalled our argument about the leaves. When was that? Last year? Two years ago? I had a case of bronchitis that wouldn't go away, the lawn was already covered with leaves, the wind was swirling them here and there. While I stood gazing out the window a great sadness came over me, the sky was black, the place looked abandoned. I went to your room, you were lying in bed with headphones attached to your ears. I asked you to please rake up the leaves. I had to repeat myself several times, louder and louder, before you heard me. You shrugged your shoulders and said, "What for? No one picks up leaves in nature, they just lie there and decay like they're supposed to." Nature was your great ally in those days, her unalterable laws helped you to justify everything you did. Instead of explaining to you that a garden is nature domesticated, a nature-dog that resembles its master more and more every year and requires constant attention, just like a real dog, I retreated into the living room without another word. Shortly afterward, when you passed by me on your way to the refrigerator, you saw I was crying but paid no attention. It was only much later, when you reemerged from your room and asked "What's for dinner?" that you noticed I was still sitting there crying. So you went to the kitchen and began bustling around. "Which would you rather," you yelled across the house, "chocolate pudding or an omelet?" You had understood that I was really upset and you were doing your best to be nice to me. The next morning I opened the shutters and saw you out on the lawn in the pouring rain, wearing the yellow oil-skin raincoat and raking the leaves. When you came back inside around nine I pretended nothing had happened; I knew you detested your generous impulses most of all.

As I looked at the flowerbeds this morning, feeling gloomy, I thought I really should call someone to remedy the slovenly state things have slid into since I got sick. I started thinking that the day I left the hospital, but I have yet to make up my mind to actually do it. Over the years I've become quite possessive about my garden, I refuse to let anyone else water the dahlias or pluck off dead leaves. It's strange, because as a young girl I was awfully bored by such puttering. Having a garden wasn't a privilege, it was a chore. All I had to do was relax my attention for a day or two and the order I had so painstakingly achieved would give way once again to disorder—and disorder bothered me more than anything. Inside of me there was no focus, no center, and I couldn't bear to see my own internal condition reflected in the external world. I should have remembered this when I asked you to rake up the leaves!

Your connection with your home and everything inside and around it is one of those things that can't be understood before you reach a certain age. At sixty or seventy you suddenly realize that your house and garden are no longer a house and garden where you happen to live for convenience or by chance or because they're beautiful; they're your house, your garden, they belong to you the way the shell belongs to the oyster that lives inside it. Your secretions have built the shell, your history is etched into its spirals, your shell-house envelops you all around, perhaps your presence there, the joys and sorrows you felt, will linger on in that space even after you die.

I didn't feel like reading yesterday evening, so I watched television. It's more accurate to say I listened to it, because I dozed off within half an hour. I heard scraps of words, the way your fellow travelers' conversation comes to you in disconnected bits and pieces when you're half asleep on the train. It was a program about contemporary religious sects. The reporters interviewed various holy men, some real, some fake, all spouting a river of words. I kept hearing the word karma, and it made me think about my high school philosophy professor.

He was young and quite a nonconformist for those days. While lecturing to us on Schopenhauer he talked a bit about Oriental philosophies and went on from there to introduce the concept of karma. I hadn't paid much attention to it at the time, the word and its meaning went in one ear and out the other. For years I had in the back of my mind a vague notion that it referred to some kind of law of retaliation, an eye for an eye, we reap as we sow, that kind of thing. I didn't think about karma or anything connected with it again until the principal of your nursery school called me in to discuss your strange conduct. You had put the entire school in an uproar. During storytelling hour, right out of the blue, you had started talking about your previous life. At first the teachers thought it was just some leftover infantile behavior. They tried to make little of your story and to trap you into contradictions. But you didn't fall for any of that, you even spoke words in a foreign language no one had ever heard of. When this happened for the third time, the principal summoned me to her office. She advised me, for your own good and for the sake of your future, to take you to a child psychologist. "She's been traumatized," she said. "It's normal for her to behave like this—she's trying to escape reality." Naturally, I never took you to any psychologist, you seemed like a happy child to me, I was inclined to believe your fantasies came not from some present malaise but from an entirely different order of things. I never pushed you to talk about these incidents, and you never felt the need to bring them up. Maybe those tales that so appalled your teachers vanished from your memory the very day you told them.

I've got the impression that it's become quite fashionable to discuss this sort of thing during the past few years. Once upon a time these were topics for the chosen few, now they're on everybody's lips. A while ago I read in a newspaper that in America there are even reincarnation awareness groups. People get together and talk about their previous existences. So a housewife might say, "I was a streetwalker in New Orleans in the nineteenth century and that's why I can't manage to be faithful to my husband." Or the racist gas-station attendant finds an excuse for his hatred in the fact that a Bantu tribe devoured him while he was on an expedition in the sixteenth century. What sorry nonsense! Having lost their own cultural roots, they construct past existences to patch up the gray uncertainties of the present. If the cycles of life have a meaning, I'm sure it's quite different from this.

After the affair at the nursery school, I got myself some books I thought might help me to understand you better. One of the essays I read said that children who remember a past life in detail are those who died premature, violent deaths. Some of your obsessions—gas pipes were leaking, everything might blow up in the next second—could not be explained by any of your childhood experiences, and so I was willing to entertain such explanations as this. When you were tired or anxious or fuddled by sleep, you were prey to irrational terrors. It wasn't bogeymen or witches or werewolves that frightened you, you were terrified that the entire universe might suddenly explode. The first few times you appeared in my room in the middle of the night, scared to death, I got up at once, comforted you, and then took you back to bed. You'd lie there holding my hand and ask for a story with a happy ending. To make sure I wouldn't say anything disturbing, you'd first describe to me exactly how you wanted the story to go, and I did nothing but repeat your instructions word for word. I'd tell the tale once, twice, three times; when I was sure you had calmed down, I'd get up to go to my room, and I'd hear your sleepy little voice asking me, "Is that how it goes? Does it really always end that way?"

But on some other nights, despite my belief that it's bad for children to sleep with old people, I didn't have the heart to send you back to bed. As soon as I sensed your presence next to the night table, I'd lie there without turning around and reassure you: "Everything's all right, nothing's going to explode, go back to your room." Then I'd pretend to fall sound asleep. I'd hear your soft breathing as you stood there unmoving for a while, then the bed would creak and you'd carefully slip in next to me and fall asleep exhausted, like a mouse finally reaching the safety of his lair after a bad fright. At dawn, to go along with the game, I'd take you in my arms—you'd be warm as toast and deep in sleep—and carry you back to your room. You hardly ever remembered anything when you woke up, you were almost always positive you'd spent the whole night in your own bed.

I'd speak gently to you when these panic attacks seized you during the day. "Don't you see how strong the house is?" I'd say. "Look how thick the walls are, how could they possibly explode?" But my attempts to reassure you were absolutely useless, you'd keep staring wide-eyed into the space in front of you and repeating, "Everything could explode." I never stopped wondering about this dread of yours. What was this explosion? Could it be the memory of your mother, of her tragic and sudden end? Did it belong to the life you had so casually described to your nursery-school teachers? Or were the two things mixed together in some inaccessible corner of your memory? Who can tell? Despite what people may say, I believe there still remains more shadow than light in the human mind. The book I was talking about also said that children who recall past lives are much more numerous in India and the Orient, in those countries where the concept itself is traditionally accepted. I have no trouble believing this. But imagine what would have happened if I had gone to my mother and begun to speak without warning in a foreign tongue, or if I had told her, "I can't stand you, I was much better off with my mama in my other life." You can be sure she'd have committed me to a lunatic asylum that very day.

Is there any way to avoid the destiny that environment and heredity impose on you? I don't know. Maybe at some point in the claustrophobic succession of generations someone succeeds in glimpsing a slightly higher step and tries to reach it with all his might. Snapping a link, letting fresh air into the room—I think this is the tiny secret of the cycles of life. Tiny but wearisome, and frightening in its uncertainty.

My mother married at sixteen, at seventeen she gave birth to me. In all my childhood—no, in all my life—I never saw her make a single affectionate gesture. She hadn't married for love. No one had forced her to marry, she had forced herself, mostly because she was rich and coveted a noble title, even though she was a Jewess and converted to boot. My father was an older man, a music-loving baron who had been charmed by her singing talents. Having procreated the heir that the family's good name required, they lived the rest of their days consumed by spite and petty vendettas. My mother died unsatisfied and holding a grudge, and the notion that some of the fault might lie with her never crossed her mind. The cruel world was at fault for not having offered her better choices. I was very different from her, and by the time I was seven, past the total dependence of early childhood, I couldn't stand her.

I suffered a lot because of her. She was constantly agitated, always and only about superficial things. Her alleged "perfection" made me feel I was bad, and the price I paid was alienation. In the beginning I made various attempts to be like her, but they were awkward and always ended in disaster. The more I tried, the uneasier I felt. Denying your own identity leads to self-contempt, and it's a short step from self-contempt to anger. Once I realized that my mother's love was concerned solely with appearances, with who I should be rather than who I really was, I began to hate her, in the secrecy of my room and in my secret heart.

To escape these feelings I took refuge in a world all my own. At night in my bed, I'd cover the lamp with a cloth and read adventure books into the wee hours. I loved daydreaming. I went through a period when I dreamed of being a pirate on the China Sea, a special kind of pirate who gave away all her ill-gotten gains to the poor. Outlaw fantasies eventually gave way to more altruistic fantasies; I thought I'd become a doctor and go to Africa to care for little black children. When I was fourteen, I read Schliemann's biography and realized I'd never be able to care for the sick because my true passion was archaeology. Of all the innumerable careers I imagined myself undertaking, I still believe this would have been the only right choice for me.

And in fact, in order to make my dream come true I fought my first and only battle against my father: I wanted him to send me to a high school for classical studies. It was out of the question, he said, and pointless besides, if I really wanted to study I should learn modern languages. In the end, however, I got my way, and I left middle school certain of complete victory. I was fooling myself. After I finished high school, I announced my intention to attend the university in Rome. My father's response was peremptory: "I don't want to talk about it," and as was the custom in those days, I obeyed without a murmur. Young people often think that winning a single battle means you've won the war; that's a mistake. Thinking it over now, I believe that my father would have given in eventually if I had put up a fight, if I had really dug in my heels. His categorical refusal was in line with the education system of the time. No one really believed that young people were capable of making their own decisions. Consequently, when they demonstrated independent thinking, they had to be put to the proof. For my parents, my capitulation at the first obstacle was clear evidence that what I had wasn't a genuine vocation but a passing fancy.

As far as my father and mother were concerned,

children were first and foremost a social duty. They neglected my inner development, and at the same time they were extremely rigid about the most banal aspects of good manners. I had to sit up straight at table with my elbows against my sides. If as I did so all my thoughts were focused on the most practical way of ending my life, that wasn't important. Appearances were all that counted; everything else was improper.

And so I grew up with the sense that I was some sort of ape that must be carefully trained, not a human being with her own joys and disappointments and need to be loved. Dissatisfaction soon produced a great loneliness in me, a loneliness that grew to envelop me as time passed, like a vacuum I moved in with a diver's slow, awkward gestures. Loneliness also came from the questions I asked myself and couldn't answer. Already by the age of five or six I would look around and wonder, Why am I here? Where do I come from, where do all the things I see around me come from, what's behind it all, has everything always been here even when I wasn't, will they go on forever? I was asking all the questions that sensitive children ask when they begin to glimpse the complexity of the world. I firmly believed that grown-ups asked themselves these questions too, and that furthermore they knew the answers. After two or three tries with mother and nanny, however, I realized that they not only didn't know the answers, the questions had never even occurred to them.

So my feeling of alienation increased, you see. I had to figure out every problem without help. The more time passed, the more I wondered about everything, my questions kept getting bigger, more terrible, it frightened me just to think about them.

I had my first encounter with death when I was six. My father had a hunting dog named Argus, a gentle, affectionate creature who was my favorite playmate. I'd spend entire afternoons feeding him mud-and-grass pies, or sometimes I'd be a hairdresser and make him play the client, and he'd wander about the garden uncomplainingly with hairpins adorning his ears. But one day, just as I was trying out a new hairdo on him, I noticed a swelling on his throat. For a few weeks he hadn't been running and jumping around the way he used to—he'd even stopped standing in front of me and sighing hopefully whenever I had a snack.

One morning I came home from school and he wasn't waiting for me at the gate. At first I thought he'd gone somewhere with my father. But when I saw my father calmly sitting in his study, with no Argus at his feet, I started getting very worried. I went outside and shouted my throat raw calling him all over the garden, then I went back inside and searched the house from top to bottom two or three times. That night, when I went to give my parents the obligatory goodnight kiss, I summoned up all my courage and asked my father, "Where's Argus?" "Argus," he said, without lifting his eyes from his newspaper. "Argus has gone away." "But why?" I asked. "Because he was tired of the tricks you played on him."

Tactlessness? Shallowness? Sadism? What kind of answer was that? The moment I heard those words, something broke inside of me. I stopped being able to sleep at night, and during the day any trivial thing was enough to make me burst into tears. After a month or two a pediatrician was called in. "The child is exhausted," he said, and gave me a dose of cod liver oil. Nobody ever asked me why I couldn't sleep, nor why I always carried Argus's gnawed ball around with me.

By my reckoning, that episode marked my entrance into the adult world. At six years old? Yes, at six years old. Argus had gone away because I had been a bad girl, therefore my behavior was no longer neutral; it influenced my surroundings, it destroyed things, it made them disappear.

In my terror of making another mistake, I gradually became apathetic, hesitant, less active. At night I clutched the ball in my hands and wept, saying, "Argus, please come back, even if I did something wrong I love you more than everything." When my father brought home another puppy, I didn't even want to look at it. I wanted it to stay as it was, a complete stranger.

Hypocrisy governed the rearing of children in those days. I well remember a time when I was out walking with my father and I found a dead robin under a hedge. I wasn't afraid, I picked it up and showed it to him. "Put it down!" he shouted at once. "Don't you see it's sleeping?" Death, like love, was a subject not to be addressed. Wouldn't it have been a thousand times better for them to tell me that Argus had died? My father could have taken me in his arms and said, "He was sick, I had to kill him to put him out of his misery. He's much happier where he is now." Of course I would have cried even more, I would have been inconsolable, for months I would have visited his grave, I would have talked on and on to him as he lay there under the ground. Then, slowly but surely, I would have begun to forget, I would have developed other passions, and Argus would have slipped to the back of my mind as a memory, a lovely childhood memory. Instead, Argus became a little dead thing that I still carry around inside me.

That's why I say I became an adult at six years old, because at that age my joy was replaced by anxiety, my curiosity gave way to indifference. Were my parents monsters? No, absolutely not. They were, for their time, perfectly normal.

It was only in her old age that my mother began telling me some things about her childhood. She was still a little girl when her own mother died. There had been another child, an older brother who died of pneumonia at the age of three. She'd been conceived shortly afterward, and she had the misfortune to be born not only female but on the very anniversary of her brother's demise. To recall this unhappy coincidence, she was dressed in mourning even before she was weaned. Over her cradle loomed a large portrait of her brother, painted in oils; every time she opened her eyes, it served to remind her that she was just a replacement, a washed-out copy of someone better. Do you understand? How could she be blamed for her coldness, her foolish choices, her total aloofness? And if we could go even further back and observe her mother, or her mother's mother, who knows what else we'd discover.

Unhappiness is generally transmitted through the female line, passing from mother to daughter the way some genetic abnormalities do. And instead of diminishing as it passes, it steadily grows more intense, more ineradicable and profound. That era was very different for men; they had their professions, their politics, their wars, they had outlets for their energy. Not us. For countless generations we've been confined to the bedroom, the kitchen, and the bathroom; we've taken millions of steps, made millions of gestures, each one encumbered by the same rancor and the same dissatisfaction. Have I become a feminist? No, don't worry, I'm just trying to see clearly what's behind all this.

Do you remember how every August we used to go out on the promontory to watch the fireworks over the ocean during *Ferragosto?* Every now and then we saw one that exploded before it got very high. Well, whenever I think about my mother's life, or my grandmother's, or the lives of so many people I know, that's the image that comes to mind—fireworks that fizzled down in the lower altitudes instead of climbing up to the sky.

November 21

I'VE READ somewhere that Manzoni, while he was writing *I promessi sposi,* would get up every morning delighted to rejoin his characters. I can't say the same for myself. Though so many years have passed, it still gives me no pleasure to talk about my family, my mother has remained in my memory as motionless and hostile as a janissary. This morning, in an attempt to put a little fresh air between her and me, between me and my memories, I went for a walk in the garden. It had rained during the night. Toward the west the sky was clear, but purple clouds were still looming behind the house. I went back inside just before another shower started. This soon became a thunderstorm, the house was so dark I had to turn on the lights. I unplugged the TV and the refrigerator so lightning wouldn't damage them, then I put the flashlight in my pocket and went to the kitchen for our daily get-together.

As soon as I sat down, however, I realized I wasn't ready yet, maybe there was too much electricity in the air, my thoughts were flying here and there like sparks. So I got up and wandered around the house for a bit, with the intrepid Buck at my heels and no precise destination in mind. I went into the room where I used to sleep with your grandfather, then into the room I use now (it was your mother's), then into the long-neglected dining room, and finally into your room. As I moved about, I remembered the impression the house made on me the first time I entered it: I didn't like it at all. I hadn't picked it out; my husband Augustus had, and in haste at that. We needed a place to live and couldn't wait any longer. Since it was big enough and had a garden, he figured it met all our requirements. The moment we opened the gate I thought the place was in bad taste, or rather in the worst possible taste. No single part of it went with any other part, whether in shape or in color. From one side it looked like a Swiss chalet, on the other the big round window and the stepped roof made it resemble one of those Dutch houses that face canals. If you saw it from a distance, with those seven chimneys, all different, you knew it could only exist in a fairy tale. It was built in the twenties, but none of its particulars made you think so. Its lack of an identity distressed me, it took me years to get used to the idea that it was mine, that my family's existence was contained within its walls.

While I was standing in your room lightning struck nearby and blew out all the lights. Instead of switching on the flashlight, I lay down on the bed. Outside there was the roaring rain and the lashing wind, inside there were various sounds, creaks, little thuds, the groans of wood under stress. I closed my eyes for a second and the house seemed like a ship, a great sailing ship navigating across the lawn. The storm didn't let up until lunchtime, I looked out of your window and saw that two big branches from the walnut tree were down.

Now I'm back in the kitchen, my old battleground, I've eaten and washed up my few dishes. Buck's sleeping at my feet, knocked out by this morning's excitement. The older he gets, the more thunderstorms terrorize him to the point where it's hard for him to recover.

One of the books I bought when you were going to nursery school said that your former lives determine what family you're born into. We have that particular mother and that particular father because only they will make it possible for us to understand a bit more, to take a tiny step forward. But if it's like that, I wondered, why do things stand still for so many generations? Why do we turn back instead of going on?

According to an article I read recently in the scientific supplement of some newspaper, it's possible that evolution doesn't work the way we've always thought it did. The latest theories suggest that changes don't occur gradually. Longer claws or a more versatile beak don't take shape slowly, millimeter by millimeter, generation after generation. No, they appear suddenly; between the mother and her child everything has changed, everything's different. Skeletal remains—such as jawbones, hooves, skulls with different teeth—confirm this. Intermediate forms have never been found for a great many species. Grandfather's like this, his grandson's like that, there's been a leap between one generation and the next. What if the interior lives of people worked like this too?

Changes accumulate stealthily, they're slow, slow, and then one day they explode. Suddenly someone breaks the circle, decides to be different. Fate, heredity, upbringing, where does one begin and the other end? Stop and ponder this mystery for a moment and you'll be dismayed.

Shortly before I got married, my father's sister

—the spiritualist—had an astrologer friend cast my horoscope. One day she accosted me with a sheet of paper in her hand and said, "Here you are, this is your future." It was a geometrical drawing, lots of planets and lines and interesting angles. I remember thinking at the time that there was no harmony in it, no continuity, just a series of jumps and swerves so sharp they seemed out of control. On the back the astrologer had written: "A difficult path, you'll have to arm yourself with every virtue before you can follow it to the end."

I was deeply struck by this. Up to that point my life had seemed awfully banal, I had certainly had problems, but they hadn't seemed all that serious, adolescent cracks rather than gaping chasms. Even later, as a grown-up, wife, mother, widow, and grandmother, I always retained this apparent normalcy. The only extraordinary event, if it can be called that, was your mother's tragic death. Looking closely at my life, though, I can see that that star chart didn't lie. Beneath the solid, regular surface, the humdrum routines of a middle-class lady, there was constant movement, all the little triumphs, the lacerations, the sudden darknesses, and the bottomless abysses. I've often been desperate in my life, I've felt like a soldier marking time but never going anywhere. Times changed, people changed, everything around me changed, and it seemed to me I stayed the same.

Your mother's death put an end to my monotonous marching in place. My opinion of myself, which was already rather modest, collapsed in a single instant. Maybe I had made a tiny bit of progress, I told myself, but now I was going backward, I'd reached a new low. There were days when I thought I wouldn't make it, it seemed to me that the minimal understanding I'd acquired so far had been canceled out in a single blow. Luckily, I couldn't wallow in this depression very long; life went on, and so did its demands.

Life was you. When you arrived you were small, defenseless. You had no one but me in the world, and you invaded this sad, silent house with your sudden laughter and your tears. I remember watching your big baby head swaying between the table and the sofa and thinking, Well, it's not all over yet. Because of the unpredictable generosity of chance, I had been given another try.

Chance. Mrs. Morpurgo's husband once told me this word doesn't exist in Hebrew. If you want to talk about something in terms of chance you have to resort to the word hazard, which is Arabic. Funny, don't you think? Funny but also reassuring: where God is, there's no room for chance, not even for the humble sound that represents it. Everything is ordered and regulated from on high, everything that happens to you happens for a reason. I've always greatly envied people who em-

brace this vision of the universe without hesitating
—for them the choice is easy. As for me, despite a
great deal of goodwill, I've never succeeded in seeing things this way for more than two days in a
row. I always backslide when I consider the horror
and injustice in the world; I can't justify them and
give thanks, I'm always filled with rebellious anger.

And now I'm going to commit a really hazard-
ous action: I'm going to send you a kiss. I know,
you hate kisses, right? They ricochet off your shell
like tennis balls. But that makes no difference, I'm
sending you a kiss whether you like it or not, you
can't do anything about it, there it goes, it's light
and transparent and flying over the ocean.

I'm tired. I've reread everything up to here, rather
anxiously. Will you understand any of it? I've got
such a crowd of things in my head, they want to
get out and they're pushing one another like ladies
at an end-of-season sale. I can never organize my
thoughts so that they move in a logical progression
from beginning to end. Sometimes I wonder
whether it's because I never went to college. I've
read many books, I've been curious about lots of
things, but always with one thought for the
diapers, another for the stove, a third for my feelings. A botanist walking through a field picks
flowers in an ordered way, he knows what inter-

ests him and what doesn't; he selects, discards, determines relationships. But a day-tripper in the same field uses a different method, he chooses one flower because it's yellow, another because it's blue, the next one because of its scent, and the one after that because it happens to be growing beside the path. I believe this is the way I've gone about gathering knowledge. Your mother was constantly giving me a hard time about that. Whenever we started any kind of discussion, I'd surrender almost immediately. "You can't argue at all," she told me. "Like all the bourgeoisie, you don't know how to make a serious defense of what you believe."

Just as you're driven by some wild restlessness no one can name, so was your mother driven by ideology. For her the fact that I talked about small matters instead of great ones was reason enough to reprimand me. She called me a reactionary, said I was diseased with bourgeois fantasies. From her point of view I was rich, therefore dedicated to superfluous luxury and naturally inclined to evil.

From the way she looked at me sometimes I was certain that if there had been a people's tribunal with her presiding, she would have sentenced me to death. I was guilty of living in a fair-sized house with a garden instead of a hovel or a suburban tenement. Not only that, I had inherited a small income that we both lived on. By way of avoiding the mistakes my own parents had made, I took (or at least I tried to take) an interest in what she said. I never ridiculed her, and I never let her see how alien her totalitarian ideas were to me, though I'm sure she knew I shrank from her parroted ready-made phrases.

Ilaria went to the University of Padua. She could easily have gone to Trieste, but she was too intolerant to continue living with me. If I suggested visiting her, the reply was hostile silence. Her studies progressed quite slowly. I didn't know who she lived with, she never would tell me. I was worried, because I knew how susceptible she was. This was 1968, the time of the May riots in Paris, the radical student movements, the occupied universities. Listening to her infrequent telephone reports, I realized I just couldn't follow her anymore, she was always fervent about something and that something kept changing all the time. I played my maternal part, I tried to understand her, but it was extremely difficult. Everything was frenetic, elusive, there were too many new ideas, too many absolutes. Instead of using her own words, Ilaria spoke in chains of slogans, one after another. I was concerned for her mental stability and worried by the way her natural tendency to be arrogant was receiving reinforcement from this sense of belonging to a group of people who shared the same certainties and the same rigid dogmas.

November 21

During her sixth year at the university, an unusually long silence worried me so much I took a train and went to visit her. I had never done this in all the time she'd been in Padua. She was appalled when she opened the door; instead of greeting me, she attacked me. "Who invited you?" she asked, but she didn't wait for an answer. "You should have warned me, I'm just about to leave. I have a big exam this morning." Since she still had her nightshirt on, she was obviously lying. I pretended not to notice and said, "Never mind, in that case I'll wait and we'll celebrate your success together." Shortly afterward she really did leave, in such a hurry that she left her books on the table.

When I found myself alone in her apartment I did what any other mother would have done. I started rummaging through drawers, looking for a sign that might help me understand what direction her life had taken. I had no intention of spying on her or censuring her, I wasn't interested in conducting an inquisition, I've never gone in for such things. I just had this terrible anxiety, and I couldn't calm down until I discovered some point of contact. Except for flyers and pamphlets of revolutionary propaganda, I found nothing, no letters, no diary. There was a poster on her bedroom wall with these words: "The family is airy and stimulating. Like a gas chamber." In its way, that was a clue.

Ilaria came back in the early afternoon, looking as exhausted as when she left. "How did the exam go?" I asked, in the most affectionate tone possible. She shrugged. "Same as all the others," she said, and after a while she added, "Is that why you're here to check on me?" I wanted to avoid a clash, so I quietly and amenably replied that I had only one desire, to talk with her a little.

"Talk?" she repeated incredulously. "About what? Your mystical flights?"

"About you, Ilaria," I said softly, trying to meet her eyes. She kept them fixed on a weeping willow well past its prime as she stepped closer to the window. "I've got nothing to say, not to you, anyway. I don't want to waste my time with confidential bourgeois chitchat." Then she moved her eyes from the willow to her wristwatch and said, "It's late, I've got an important meeting. You'll have to leave." I didn't mind her, instead of walking out I went to her and took her hands in mine. "What's going on?" I asked. "What's making you suffer?" I heard her breathing quicken. "It hurts my heart to see you in such a state," I added. "Even if you reject me as a mother, I don't reject you as a daughter. I want to help you, but if you don't meet me halfway I can't do it." At that point her chin started trembling the way it used to do when she was a little girl and on the verge of tears. She jerked her hands away from me and spun around to face the wall. Her thin, tense body was racked by deep sobs. I stroked her hair; her head was fiery hot, just as her hands had been icy cold. She whipped back around and embraced me, hiding her face against my shoulder. "Mama," she said, "I . . . I . . ."

At that precise moment the telephone rang.

"Let it ring," I whispered into her ear.

"I can't," she replied, drying her eyes.

When she lifted the receiver her voice was once again metallic and aloof. I gathered from her brief conversation that something serious must have happened. In fact, as soon as she hung up, she said, "I'm sorry, but now you really have to go." We went out together, at the door she let herself go for a second and gave me a swift, guilty hug. "No one can help me," she whispered as she squeezed me. I walked with her the few steps to where her bicycle was chained. She straddled it, slipped two fingers under my necklace, and said, "The pearls, right? Your special permit. You haven't had the nerve to take a step without them since the day you were born!"

After so many years, that's the episode with your mother that I remember most. I brood over it often. How is it possible, I ask myself, that of all the experiences we shared, this particular one always comes to mind first? Just today, when I was going over it for the ten thousandth time, I recalled an old saying, "The tongue probes where the tooth aches." You may wonder what that has to do with it. A lot, believe me. That episode keeps coming back to me because it was the only time I had the possibility of making a change. Your mother was in tears, embracing me; for a moment there was an opening in her shell, a tiny crack I could have passed through, and once inside I could gradually have made more room for myself. I could have become a fixed point in her life, but doing this would have required great determination. When she told me, "You really must go," I should have stayed. I should have taken a room in a nearby hotel, gone back daily to knock on her door, kept trying until that crack became a passage. I was close, I could feel it.

And instead I didn't act. Out of cowardice, laziness, and a false sense of propriety, I did what she told me to do. I had detested my own mother's intrusions, I wanted to be a different sort of mother and let Ilaria have her independence. Such high-mindedness often masks a lack of real caring, a desire not to get involved. It's a fine, fine line, crossing it or not is the work of a moment, it's a decision you make or you don't. You realize its importance only after your moment has passed. Only then do you feel regret, only then do you understand that in that instant intervention was imperative, not scruples about independence. Love doesn't suit the lazy, sometimes it requires strong, precise actions. Do you see? I disguised my listless cowardice as noble sentiments about personal liberty.

The idea of destiny comes to one with the years. In general, nobody your age ever thinks about it, you see everything that happens as the result of your own will. You feel like a highway worker laying out the road you have to travel down, stone by stone. It's only much later that you notice the road's already there, someone else has marked it out for you, all you have to do is go forward. One usually makes this discovery around forty, that's when you start to realize that things don't depend on you alone. It's a dangerous moment; many people slide into a kind of claustrophobic fatalism. You'll have to let more years pass before you can recognize the reality of destiny. Around the age of sixty, when the road at your back is longer than the one in front of you, you see something you've never seen before: the road you've traveled wasn't straight, but forking constantly, at every step there was a turning, an arrow indicating a new direction —a footpath veering off on one side, a grassy lane disappearing into the woods on the other. You've taken some of those side roads without noticing it, and there are others you didn't even see; you don't know where the roads you passed by would have taken you, or whether they would have led you someplace better or worse; you don't know, but that doesn't stop you from feeling regret. You could have done something and you didn't, you turned back instead of going on. Do you remember playing Snakes and Ladders? Well, life proceeds in much the same way.

At the forks in your road you encounter other lives. Getting to know them or not, merging with them or passing them by, depends solely on the choice you make in a moment; though you may not know it, your whole life and the lives of those close to you are at stake when you choose whether to go straight or turn aside.

November 22

THE WEATHER changed last night, the east wind came up and swept away all the clouds in a few hours. Before I got down to writing I took a stroll in the garden. The wind was still blowing strong, it got right under my clothes. Buck was ecstatic, he wanted to play, he was trotting beside me with a pinecone in his mouth. With my puny strength I managed to throw it for him only once, it had a very short flight, but he was content all the same. After checking your rose's health, I went to say hello to the walnut tree and the cherry tree, my two favorites.

Remember how you used to tease me when you

saw me stroking one of our trees? "What are you doing?" you'd say. "That's not a horse." When I pointed out that touching a tree is no different from touching any other living thing, in fact even better, you'd shrug and go away miffed. Why is it better? Because if I scratch Buck's head, for example, I do indeed feel something warm and vibrant, but beneath that there's always a tremor of agitation. Perhaps dinnertime is coming soon, or not soon enough; perhaps he's longing for you or just recalling a bad dream. Do you see? Dogs, like people, have too many thoughts, too many requirements. Neither dog nor man can attain peace and happiness by himself alone.

Trees are different. From the moment it sprouts until the day it dies, a tree stays fixed in the same spot. Its roots are nearer than anything else to the heart of the earth, and its crown is nearer to the sky. Sap courses through it from top to bottom, from bottom to top. It expands and contracts according to the daylight. It waits for rain, it waits for sun, it waits for one season and then another, it waits for death. Not one of the things that enable it to live depends on its will. It exists and that's all. Now do you see why trees are so good to stroke? Because they stand so staunchly, because their breathing is so slow and so serene and so very deep. Somewhere in the Bible it's written that God has wide nostrils. This may be a bit irreverent, but every time I try to imagine a visible form for the Divine Being what I see in my mind's eye is an oak tree.

We had one where I lived as a child, it was so big it took two people to embrace its trunk. Starting when I was four or five, I loved to go and visit it. I'd sit there, feeling the damp grass under my bottom and the fresh wind on my face and in my hair. I'd breathe deeply and know that there was a higher order of things and that I and everything I could see belonged to it. Even though I knew nothing about music, something inside me was singing. I couldn't tell you what kind of melody it was, there wasn't any definite tune or refrain, it was more like the regular, powerful rhythm of a bellows breathing somewhere near my heart; and this breath pervaded me, body and mind, shining like light and singing like music. I was happy to be alive, I was conscious of nothing but my happiness.

Maybe it will seem strange or abnormal to you that a child should have such intuitions. Unfortunately, we're used to thinking of childhood as a period of blindness and inadequacy, not as the richest time of all. And yet, to convince yourself that it's so all you have to do is look carefully into the eyes of a newborn baby. Try it if you get the chance, forget preconceptions and observe the child closely. How do his eyes seem to you? Empty, unconscious? Or ancient, distant, wise?

Babies naturally know how to breathe deeply, it's we adults who have lost this ability. At the age of four or five I had as yet learned nothing about God or religion, nor about any of the fine messes people have made in their name.

You know, when it came time to decide whether you should take religious classes in school, I couldn't make up my mind. On the one hand I remembered the catastrophe of my own collision with dogmas, on the other I was absolutely convinced that education should cultivate not only the mind but the spirit too. The problem eventually solved itself on the day your first hamster died. You held it in your hand and looked up at me, thoroughly perplexed. "Where is he now?" you asked. I answered by repeating your question: "Where do you think he is?" Do you remember how you replied? "He's in two places. Part of him is here, the other part is up in the clouds." We buried him with a little funeral ceremony that same afternoon. You knelt in front of the tiny mound of earth and said a prayer: "Be happy, Tony. We'll be together again one day."

Maybe I never mentioned it, but I had my first five years of school with the sisters at the Sacred Heart Academy. Believe me when I tell you that this did more than slight damage to my little brain, which was already in something of a spin. The sisters kept a huge crèche set up all year long in the entryway to the school. There was Baby Jesus in his manger, his father, his mother, the ox, and the ass, and all around the stable were papier-mâché mountains and precipices populated only by a flock of little sheep. Each sheep stood for a pupil, and it got moved closer to or farther from Jesus' stall according to how we behaved during the day. We passed the crèche every morning on our way to our classrooms, and so we were forced to look at our positions. On the side opposite the stable there was a deep, deep chasm, and all the worst sheep stood on its edge with two little hooves already dangling over the void. Between the ages of six and ten the steps my lamb took determined the conditions of my life. And I don't have to tell you she hardly ever moved away from the rim of the precipice.

In my heart, with all the willpower I had, I tried to respect the commandments I'd been taught. I did it because of the natural desire to conform that children have, but not only that: I was genuinely convinced that one ought to be good, not lie, not be conceited. I was nevertheless always on the verge of falling. Why? For stupid things. When I went in tears to the mother superior to find out the reason why I'd been moved for the umpteenth time, she'd tell me, "Because the bow you wore yesterday was too big . . . Because one of your classmates heard you singing to yourself as you left the school . . . Because you didn't wash your hands before going to the table." See what I mean? Once again my offenses had to do with superficial things, just like the ones my mother accused me of. Our teachers didn't care about inner coherence, only outward conformity. One day, when I had wound up on the very edge of the chasm, I burst into sobs and said, "But I love Baby Jesus." And do you know what the nun standing there said to me? "So you're not just messy but a liar to boot. If you really loved Baby Jesus, you'd keep your notebooks in better order." And snap, she flicked her finger and sent my little sheep plunging down into the abyss.

I believe I didn't sleep for two whole months after that. As soon as I closed my eyes I felt the mattress under my back burst into flames, and horrible voices sneered, "Just wait, we're coming to get you!" Naturally I never told a shred of any of this to my parents. When she saw me sallow-faced and nervous my mother would say, "The child is exhausted," and I'd hold my breath and swallow one tablespoon of tonic after the other.

Who knows how many sensitive, intelligent people have turned their backs on spiritual matters forever because of episodes like this? Every time I hear someone say how wonderful their school days were, how they still regret their passing, it just leaves me speechless. As far as I'm concerned, that was one of the worst periods of my life, maybe even the absolute all-time worst considering the sense of impotence I always felt. Throughout the years of elementary school there was a ferocious battle going on within me between my desire to remain faithful to what I felt inside and the wish to accept what the others believed, even though I sensed instinctively that it was false.

It's strange, but now when I relive those old emotions I have the impression that the great crisis of my growing up didn't happen during adolescence, as it does with everyone else, but during those early childhood years. By the time I was twelve, thirteen, fourteen, I already possessed a gloomy stability of my very own. The great metaphysical questions had slowly receded into the background, replaced by new, harmless fantasies. I went to mass with my mother on Sundays and holy days, I knelt with much show of contrition to receive the host, but while I did so I'd be thinking about other things: this was just one of the little performances I had to put on in exchange for a quiet life. That's why I never signed you up for religious instruction and never regretted my decision. When your childish curiosity prompted questions on the subject, I tried to give you direct, objective answers, without leaving out any of the sense of mystery we all share. And when you stopped asking questions, I discreetly avoided bringing up the matter again. This is one of those areas where you can't push or pull too hard, otherwise the same thing happens to you as happens to street vendors: the more they hustle their products, the more the whole thing seems like a hoax. With you, I simply tried not to snuff out what was already there. For the rest I waited.

But don't think my path was always so smooth. Although at the age of four I had felt the breath that inspires all things, by the time I was seven I'd already forgotten it. At first, it's true, I still heard the music, it was in the background but it was there. It seemed like a stream rushing through a mountain gorge, if I stood still at the edge of the cliff and listened I managed to hear the sound. But eventually the stream was transformed into an old radio on the blink. One minute the music was deafening, the next minute I couldn't hear a thing.

My father and mother missed no opportunity to scold me for my singing habit. Once during dinner I even got slapped—my first slap—because of a bit of unconscious warbling. "No singing at table!" my father thundered. "No singing if you're not a singer," my mother chimed in. I was crying, and I said through my tears, "But I hear singing inside me." For my parents, anything that wasn't part of the concrete, material world was absolutely incomprehensible. So how could I possibly hold on to my music? Maybe I could have if I'd been destined for sainthood, but my destiny was in fact cruelly normal.

Slowly but surely the music disappeared, and with it the deep sense of joy that had accompanied me in my first years. You know, that's what I've regretted the most, that joy. Of course, later there were times when I felt happy, but happiness is to joy as an electric light bulb is to the sun. Happiness always has an object, you're happy because of something, it's a condition whose existence depends on external things. Joy, on the other hand, has no object. It seizes you for no apparent reason, it's like the sun, its burning is fueled by its own heart.

In the course of the years I abandoned my self, the deepest part of me, in order to become another person, the one my parents expected me to become. I shed my personality and acquired a character. You'll no doubt find out for yourself that the world prizes character much more than personality.

Contrary to popular opinion, character and personality never go together; in fact, the former generally drives out the latter once and for all. My mother, for example, had a strong character, she was secure about everything she did and there was nothing, absolutely nothing, that could dent that security. I was her exact opposite. There wasn't a single aspect of everyday life that sent me into raptures. I shilly-shallied before every choice, I delayed so long that finally those around me lost patience and decided for me.

Don't think it was a natural process for me to leave my personality behind and put on a character. Something deep inside me continued to rebel; one part of me wanted me to keep on being myself, while the other part, the part that wanted to be loved, tried to comply with the world's demands. I detested my mother and the superficial, empty manner she had. I detested her, and yet slowly, against my will, I was becoming just like her. This is the great, terrible blackmail of every upbringing, the one it's just about impossible to escape. No child can live without love. That's why we follow the model prescribed to us, even if we don't like it at all, even if we think it's wrong. The effects of this transaction persist into adulthood. When you become a mother it resurfaces whether you want it to or not, you may not even notice it, but it's shaping your actions once again. So when your mother was born, I was absolutely convinced I'd behave differently. And in fact I did, but the differences were superficial and completely false. To avoid imposing on your mother a model like the one that had been imposed on me at a tender age, I always left her free to make choices, I wanted her to feel she had my approval in everything she did, I constantly told her, "We're two different people and each of us must respect the other's differences."

There was a mistake in all this, a serious mistake. Do you know what it was? It was my lack of identity. Even though I was now an adult, I wasn't secure about anything. I wasn't able to love myself or have esteem for myself. Thanks to the subtle, opportunistic sensitivity that characterizes children, your mother perceived this almost immediately: she sensed that I was weak, vulnerable, easily subdued. The image I see in my mind's eye as I think about our relationship is a tree infested by a climbing vine. The tree is older, taller, it's been there a good while and has much deeper roots. The vine sprouts at its foot in a single season, it has barbs and tendrils rather than roots. There are tiny suckers on each tendril, and that's how the vine climbs up the trunk. After a year or two, it's already reached the top of the tree. While its host is losing its leaves, the parasite climber stays green. It keeps spreading, keeps putting out more tendrils, finally it covers the tree entirely and has the sun and rain all to itself. Then the tree dries up and dies; only the unfortunate trunk remains, still supporting the climber.

After her tragic death I didn't think about her for several years. Sometimes I'd realize I'd forgotten her and accuse myself of cruelty. There was you to keep up with, it's true, but I don't think that was the real reason, or maybe it was in part. My sense of defeat was too enormous for me to be able to admit it. It's only been during the last few years, since you began growing apart from me and trying to find your own way, that I've started thinking about your mother again, so much so it's become an obsession. My greatest regret is that I never had the courage to stand up to her, that I didn't just say, "You're dead wrong, you're doing something stupid." I knew those slogans she used were terribly dangerous, I knew I should put an immediate stop to that sort of thing for her own good, and nevertheless I refrained from intervening. Laziness wasn't the problem, I knew that the subjects we were discussing were absolutely essential. The reason why I acted—or failed to act—as I did was the attitude my mother taught me. In order to be loved I had to avoid arguments and pretend to be what I wasn't. Ilaria was naturally overbearing, she had more character than I did, and I feared an open confrontation, I was afraid to contradict her. If I had really loved her I would have reacted indignantly, I would have been hard on her; I should have made her do some things and stop doing others completely. Maybe that was just what she wanted, what she needed from me.

Can anyone say why elementary truths are the most difficult to understand? If I had realized at the time that the primary quality of love is strength, events probably would have unfolded differently. But in order to be strong, you have to love yourself; and in order to love yourself you need thorough self-knowledge, you have to know everything about yourself, including your most hidden secrets, the ones most difficult to accept. How can you manage to carry out a project of those dimensions while life with all its clamoring is dragging you on? If you have extraordinary gifts, you can pull it off right from the start. Ordinary mortals like your mother and me must resign themselves to the fate of dead branches and plastic containers. Someone, or maybe the wind, suddenly flings you into the river; since you're made of light material, you float instead of sinking; this seems like a victory to you and so all at once you start racing; you're dashing along wherever the current may take you; every now and then roots or rocks bring you to a halt; you're caught there for a time while the water bashes you, then it rises and frees you, you continue on; you float on the surface when the stream flows smoothly, when it passes the rapids you go under; you don't know where you're going, you've never even wondered; along the quieter stretches you can see the landscape, the banks, the bushes; more than details, you see shapes and colors, you're going too fast to see anything else; time passes, miles pass, then the banks get lower, the river broadens out, it's still in a channel but not for long. "Where am I going?" you wonder, and in that very instant you reach the sea.

Most of my life has been like this. I didn't swim, I floundered. With uncertain, confused movements, without elegance or joy, I've barely managed to keep myself afloat.

Why am I writing you all this? These confessions are too long, too intimate, what can they mean? Maybe you're bored by now, you're probably just leafing through the pages and fuming. Where's she trying to go, you may be wondering, where's she taking me? You're right, I digress a lot, often enough I deliberately leave the main road and turn off into some narrow lane. I give the impression that I'm lost, and maybe it's not just an impression—I really am lost. But this is the only way to get to that place you're looking for so hard: the center.

Do you remember when I taught you to make pancakes? When you flip them, I told you, think about anything at all except catching them properly. If you concentrate on them while they're in the air, they're certain to land in the skillet crumpled or maybe even come down splat on the burner. It's funny, but distraction is actually necessary if you want to get to the center of things, to their heart.

But it's not my heart that's talking now, it's my

stomach. It's growling at me, and with good reason, because suppertime arrived somewhere between the trip down the river and the pancakes. I have to leave you now, but before I do I'll send you another of those kisses you hate so much.

November 29

YESTERDAY'S WINDSTORM caused some suffering: I found a victim this morning during my daily walk in the garden. Instead of simply circumnavigating the house the way I always do, today, as if prompted by my guardian angel, I went all the way to the end of the garden, back where the chicken coop used to be and the compost heap is now. Just as I was walking alongside that little wall between Walter's garden and ours, I noticed something dark on the ground. It looked like a pinecone at first, but it was moving at more or less regular intervals. I had gone out without my glasses, and I had to get practically on top of it before I was able to tell it was a young blackbird, a female. I almost broke my thighbone trying to catch her. Every time I almost had her, she hopped out of reach. If I were younger, I'd have caught her in a second, but I'm too slow for that these days. Finally I had a stroke of genius. I took the kerchief off my head and threw it over her, then I bundled her up and carried her inside. Now she's in an old shoebox—I lined it with rags and punched holes in the cover, one of them big enough for her head to poke through.

While I'm writing she's here on the table in front of me. I haven't given her anything to eat yet because she's too agitated. Seeing her agitated makes me agitated too, her terrified look embarrasses me. Suppose a fairy were to drop in on me right now, first a great blinding flash of light and then she's standing there between the refrigerator and the stove, do you know what I'd ask her for? I'd ask for King Solomon's Ring, whose magic powers enable its wearer to converse with the animal world. Then I could tell the blackbird, "Don't worry, little chicky, I may be a human being but I've got the best intentions. I'll take care of you, I'll feed you, and when you're healthy again I'll let you go."

But let's get back to us. We parted in the kitchen yesterday after my homely pancake parable, which probably irritated you no end. Young people always think that serious matters must be discussed in serious, resounding tones. A short while before you left, I found that letter you put under my pillow, the one where you tried to explain to me why you were so unhappy. Now that you're far away I can tell you that what you wrote made it clear you were indeed unhappy, but aside from that I didn't understand a thing. It was all so convoluted and obscure. I'm a simple person, I belong to an era different from the one you belong to: if something's white, I say it's white; if it's black, I say black. The ability to resolve problems comes from everyday experience, from seeing things as they really are and not the way someone else says they should be. As soon as we begin to jettison the ballast, to eliminate whatever doesn't belong to us, whatever comes from outside, we're already on the right track. Many a time I've had the impression that the books you read confuse you instead of helping you in any way—they're like escaping squid, they leave a black cloud around you.

Before you made your decision about leaving, you gave me a choice, you'd either go abroad for a year or start seeing a psychiatrist. I had a severe reaction to that, remember? You can go away for three years if you want, I said, but you're never going to a psychiatrist, not even once, not even if you pay for it yourself. You were quite struck by such an extreme attitude, because you really thought you were proposing the lesser of two evils when you suggested the psychiatrist. Even though you made no protest whatsoever, I imagine you thought I was too old or too uninformed to understand such things. If so, you were wrong. Even as a child I'd heard about Freud. One of my father's brothers was a doctor who had studied in Vienna and come into contact with Freud's theories very early on. He was enthusiastic about them, and he tried to make converts of my parents whenever he came to dinner. "You'll never convince me that if I dream about eating spaghetti it means I'm afraid of death," my mother would proclaim. "If I dream about spaghetti, that means only one thing: I'm hungry." My uncle attempted in vain to explain to her that her obstinacy was due to repression, that her terror of death was beyond question because spaghetti and worms were identical and worms were what every one of us would one day become. Guess what my mother said then? After a moment of silence, she burst out in her soprano voice: "All right, so what if I dream about macaroni?"

My encounters with psychoanalysis, however, are not limited to this childhood anecdote. Your mother was in the care of a psychiatrist—an alleged psychiatrist—for nearly ten years; she was still going to see him when she died. So I had the opportunity to follow the entire development of their relationship, day after day, although at second hand. To tell the truth, in the beginning she didn't say anything about it—such things are a matter of professional secrecy, you know. But what struck me at once, and in a very negative way, was her immediate and total feeling of dependence. By the time a single month had passed her whole life was revolving around those appointments, around whatever happened between her and that man during their hour-long sessions. Jealousy, you'll say. Maybe, it's quite possible, but that wasn't the main thing; what really distressed me was seeing her a slave to a new dependency, first politics and then the relationship with that man. Ilaria had met him during her last year in Padua, and Padua was where she went every week for her appointment. When she announced this new activity to me, I was rather perplexed, and I said, "Do you really think it's necessary to go all that way to find a good doctor?"

In one sense her decision to consult a doctor about the perpetual state of crisis she was in gave me a feeling of relief. After all, I told myself, Ilaria's decided to ask someone for help, that's already a step in the right direction. On the other hand, however, I knew how fragile she was and I was anxious about her choosing a genuinely trustworthy person. Entering into someone else's mind is always a matter of extreme delicacy. "How did you find him?" I asked. "Did someone recommend him to you?" Her only response was a shrug. Then she said, "How could you understand?" and settled into a smug silence.

Although she had her own apartment in Trieste, we were in the habit of having lunch together at least once a week. After her therapy began, we kept our conversation at those lunches completely and deliberately superficial. We talked about what was going on in the city, or about the weather; if the weather was fine and nothing was going on in the city, we ate in nearly total silence.

But by her third or fourth trip to Padua I noticed a change. Instead of both of us talking about nothing, she started asking me questions: she wanted to know everything about the past, about me, her father, our relationship. There was no affection or curiosity in her inquiries: she sounded like an interrogator, repeating the same questions over and over, insisting on minute details, casting doubts on episodes she remembered perfectly well because she'd been there too. At such times I seemed to be talking not with my daughter but with a police detective willing to go to any lengths to make me confess a crime. One day, out of patience, I said to her, "Can't you talk straight? Just tell me where you're going with all this." She gave me a slightly ironic look, picked up her fork, tapped a glass with it, and when the glass went *ping* she replied: "The only place I want to go is the end of the line. I want to know when and why you and your husband clipped my wings."

That was the last time I allowed myself to be subjected to such a barrage of questions. The following week I phoned her and invited her for lunch, but on one condition: that we could have a dialogue, not a trial.

Did I have a guilty conscience? Of course I had a guilty conscience, there were many things I should have talked to Ilaria about, but baring my innermost thoughts under the pressure of an interrogation seemed both wrong and unhealthy. If I had played the game her way, we wouldn't have initiated any new rapport between two adults; I would merely have been condemned to the role of the guilty party forever, and she would have been the victim forever, with no possibility of deliverance.

I talked to her again about her therapy several months later. By then she was retreating into seclusion with her doctor for entire weekends at a time, she had lost a lot of weight, and her speech had an element of raving in it that I'd never heard before. I told her about her grandfather's brother, about his first contacts with psychoanalysis, and then I casually asked her, "Which school does your analyst belong to?" "None," she replied, "or rather to one he founded himself."

Up to then I had been simply anxious, but from that moment on I became truly and deeply worried. I managed to find out the doctor's name, and after a brief investigation I also found out that he wasn't a doctor at all. The hopes I'd cherished in the beginning about the good effects of this therapy collapsed at a single blow. Naturally, it wasn't just his lack of a degree that made me suspicious, but his lack of a degree considered together with Ilaria's steadily deteriorating condition. If his treatment were valid, I thought, she might have had a bad time at first, but then she would have begun to improve; slowly, despite doubts and relapses, a new awareness should have dawned. But instead, little by little Ilaria had lost interest in everything else. She'd finished her studies several years before and she wasn't doing anything, she was out of touch with the few friends she used to have, her sole activity was to scrutinize the movements of her psyche with an entomologist's obsessiveness. The world revolved around what she had dreamed last night or a phrase her father or I had spoken to her twenty years ago. I could see her life was coming apart, and I felt utterly helpless.

It was only three years later that a glimmer of hope appeared for a few weeks. Shortly after Easter, I had suggested that we take a trip together. To my great surprise, Ilaria didn't reject the idea out of hand; instead she looked up from her plate and said, "Where could we go?" "I don't know," I replied. "Wherever you want, wherever we take it into our heads to go."

That very afternoon we were waiting impatiently for the travel agencies to open. We pestered them for weeks, looking for a trip we might like. In the end we opted for Greece—Crete and Santorini—in late May. All the practical tasks we had to accomplish together before leaving united us in a completely new way. She was obsessive about her luggage, terrified she might forget some absolutely indispensable item. I bought her a little notebook to calm her down. "Make a list of all the things you need," I told her. "Scratch off each item after you put it in the suitcase."

As I was going to bed that evening I regretted that I hadn't thought sooner about taking a trip together as an excellent way to set about mending our relationship. The Friday before we left Ilaria telephoned me, using her metallic voice. I believe she was calling from a pay phone. "I have to go to Padua," she said. "I'll be back Tuesday evening at the latest." "Is it really necessary?" I asked, but she'd already hung up.

I heard nothing from her until the following Thursday. The phone rang at two o'clock, she spoke in a tone that vacillated between hardheartedness and regret. "I'm sorry," she said, "but I'm not going to Greece." She was waiting for my reaction, and so was I. After a few seconds, I replied: "I'm very sorry too. However, I'm going all the same." She understood how disappointed I was and tried to justify her decision. "If I leave I'll be running away from myself," she whispered.

As you can imagine, it was a wretched vacation. I forced myself to follow the guides and be interested in landscapes and archaeology, but in reality all I was thinking about was your mother and where her life was going.

I told myself that Ilaria was like someone who plants his garden, sees the first little sprouts appear, and then is seized by the fear that something may harm them. So he douses them with plenty of insecticide to keep aphids and caterpillars at bay and buys a nice waterproof, wind-resistant plastic sheet to cover them with. His labors know no rest, night and day he thinks about his garden and how best to defend it. Then one morning he lifts the plastic sheet and gets a terrible surprise: all his plants are rotten and dead. If he'd left them to grow freely, some would've died all the same, but others would've survived. Do you see what I mean? That's the way things go, life requires generosity: cultivating your own little character while shutting your eyes to everything around you means you can keep on breathing, but you're really dead.

By imposing an excessive rigidity on her mind,

Ilaria had suppressed the voice of her heart. Our arguments left me scared even to pronounce this word. Once when she was a teenager I told her, "The heart is the center of the spirit." The next morning I found the dictionary on the kitchen table, open to the word spirit, with the definition underlined in red pencil: "colorless liquid used to preserve fruit."

Nowadays the word heart always sounds a little naive or commonplace. When I was young it could still be spoken without embarrassment, but now it's a term no one uses anymore. On the rare occasions when it gets mentioned, the reference isn't to the heart in the fullest sense of the word, but only to some malfunction, anemic tissue caused by a blocked artery, say, or problems with an auricle; there's no longer so much as a hint about the heart as the center, the essence of human nature. I've often wondered why it's been ostracized like this. "He who puts his trust in his own heart is a fool" —Augusto often used to say that, quoting the Bible. But why on earth should such a person be a fool? Is it because the heart is like a combustion chamber? Because there's darkness inside there, darkness and fire? The mind is as modern as the heart is ancient. These days people who follow their hearts are considered to be close to the animal world, to uninhibited nature, while those who follow reason are close to the upper spheres of reflection. But suppose things aren't like that, suppose they're just the opposite? Suppose it's this excess of reason that's starving our lives?

On the voyage back from Greece I got into the habit of spending part of every morning near the bridge. I liked peeking inside, looking at the radar and all that complicated equipment that told where we were going. One day I was up there watching the various antennae vibrate in the air and I thought that people are becoming more and more like radios that can tune in to only one station, rather like what happens with the miniradios you get as prizes in boxes of soap powder: although the whole range of frequencies is marked on the dial, you won't be able to pick up more than one or two stations; all the others will just keep buzzing around in the air. Well, I've got the impression that excessive use of the mind produces the same effect: we succeed in picking up only a limited portion of all the reality that surrounds us. Confusion often reigns in this small portion because it's crammed full of words, and words usually make us go round in circles instead of leading us to some higher ground.

Understanding demands silence. I didn't know this when I was young, I know it now as I roam through the house mute and solitary as a fish in a crystal bowl. Words imprison the mind; if any rhythm comes naturally to it, it's the disordered rhythm of our thoughts; but the heart breathes, it's the only organ that pulses, and those pulsations attune it to greater pulsations. Sometimes, out of absentmindedness more than anything else, I leave the television on all afternoon. Although I'm not watching it, its sound follows me through the rooms, and when I go to bed on those evenings I'm much more nervous than usual and have trouble falling asleep. Continuous noise and racket is a kind of drug, once you get used to it you can't do without it.

I don't want to go too far beyond this for now. These pages I've written today seem like a cake put together from several different recipes, all sorts of disparate ingredients all mixed up, like one of those outlandish things you had me taste one day, telling me it was called "nouvelle cuisine." Maybe I've made a huge mess. If a philosopher were to read this, I imagine he wouldn't be able to restrain himself from marking up everything with his red pencil the way my old teachers used to do. "Inconsistent," he'd write. "Not to the point. Lacking logical support."

Suppose a psychologist got hold of it! He could write a long essay on my failed relationship with my daughter, on everything I'm repressing. But even if I have repressed something, what difference can it make now? I had a daughter and I lost her. She died in a car crash, on the very day when

I revealed to her that the father who had caused her so many problems, as she said, was in fact not her real father. That day is as present in my memory as if I were watching a film, except that it isn't moving through a projector, it's fixed to a wall. I know the sequence of scenes by heart, I know the details of every scene. Nothing has slipped away from me, everything's here inside, it pulses like blood through my thoughts whether I'm awake or asleep. It will keep on pulsing even after I die.

The little blackbird's awake, she's sticking her head through the hole in her box and producing an emphatic peep at regular intervals. She seems to be saying, "I'm hungry, what's taking you so long to feed me?" I just got up and looked in the refrigerator for something that would do for her. Since there wasn't a thing, I picked up the phone to ask Walter if he had any worms. While I was dialing the number, I said to the bird, "You're a lucky little thing. You were born from an egg, and after your first flight you forgot what your parents looked like."

November 30

JUST BEFORE NINE this morning, Walter arrived with his wife and a little bag—he'd managed to get some mealworms from one of his cousins who's a fisherman. He helped me lift the blackbird very gently out of the box, her heart was beating like crazy under her soft breast feathers. I picked the worms off a saucer with a pair of tweezers and offered them to her. No matter how appetizingly I waved them in front of her beak, she wasn't interested. "Prop it open with a toothpick," Walter suggested. "You'll have to force it open with your fingers first." Naturally I didn't have the nerve to do this. Then I thought about all the little birds you and I raised together and remembered that the thing to do was to prod the beak from the side, so that's what I did. It was as if there were a spring inside, she popped her mouth open at once. After three worms she was full. Mrs. Razman put on some coffee—I haven't been able to do that with my lame hand—and we had a chat about this and that. If they weren't so kind and helpful, my life would be a lot more difficult. In a few days they're going to a nursery to buy seeds and bulbs for next spring, and they've invited me to go along. I didn't say yes or no; we agreed to talk again by phone tomorrow morning.

That day was the eighth of May. I'd spent the morning working in the garden, the columbine had bloomed and the cherry tree was covered with buds. Your mother appeared at lunchtime, unannounced. She crept up quietly behind me, then suddenly shouted "Surprise!" and scared me so much I dropped the rake. The expression on her face contradicted the fake joy of her enthusiastic exclamations. She was sallow, and her lips were pressed together. She kept running her fingers through her hair as she spoke, tugging on it, brushing it off her face, putting a hank in her mouth.

This had been her state for quite a while, so it didn't worry me, at least not any more than usual.

I asked her where you were. She told me you were playing at a friend's house. While we were walking back to the house, she pulled a crumpled bunch of forget-me-nots out of her pocket. "It's Mother's Day," she said, and then stood there looking at me with the flowers in her hand, undecided whether to make the next move. So I made it for her, I went to her and put my arms around her and thanked her affectionately, but the feel of her body against mine gave me an awful shock. There was a terrible rigidity in her, she went even stiffer when I hugged her. I had the sensation that her body was completely hollow inside, it was putting out cold air the way a cave does. I clearly remember thinking of you in that moment. What will become of the child, I wondered, with a mother who's in this sorry state? Things were getting worse instead of better as time passed; I was worried about you, about how they would affect you. Your mother was very possessive and brought you to see me as seldom as possible. She wanted to preserve you from my negative influence. Though I had ruined her life, I wouldn't succeed in ruining yours.

Since it was lunchtime, after our embrace I went to the kitchen to fix something to eat. The day was mild, so we set up the table outside, under the wisteria. I spread out the tablecloth with the little green and white checks and put a little vase with the forget-me-nots in the middle of the table. You see? I remember everything with incredible precision for someone whose memory's generally so wobbly. Was I somehow aware that that would be the last time I would see her alive? Or did I perhaps try, after her death, to find artificial ways of expanding the time we spent together? Who knows? Who can say?

I didn't have anything that was already prepared, so I put together a tomato sauce. When it was almost done I asked Ilaria what kind of pasta she wanted. She yelled back "Don't care" from outside, so I cooked some fusilli. When we were sitting down I asked a few questions about you and got evasive replies. Steady streams of insects were shuttling back and forth around us, they almost drowned out our words as they buzzed in and out of the flowers. All at once something dark dived onto your mother's plate. "It's a wasp! Kill it, kill it!" she shouted, jumping up from her chair and knocking everything over. When I leaned closer, I saw that the culprit was a bumblebee. "It's not a wasp," I told her. "It's a bumblebee, it's harmless." I shooed it away and put the pasta back on her plate. She still looked quite undone, but she sat down again, picked up her fork, toyed with it awhile, passing it from one hand to the other, then braced her elbows against the table and said, "I need some money." On the tablecloth where the fusilli had fallen there was a large red stain.

This money question had been going on for several months by then. Sometime before the previous Christmas, Ilaria had confessed to having signed some papers in favor of her analyst. When I asked for more details, she ducked as usual. "Just guarantees," she said. "A mere formality." This was her terrorist mode: when she had something to tell me, she told it halfway, thus dumping her anxiety onto me without giving me the information I'd need in order to help her. There was a subtle sadism in all this, and, beyond sadism, a raging need to always be the centerpiece of some worrisome business. Most of the time, however, these flights of hers were only dramatic performances.

She'd say, for example, "I've got cancer of the ovaries," and after a brief but desperate investigation I'd determine that she'd simply gone for a routine checkup, she'd taken that test that every woman takes. Do you see? It was a little like the boy who cried wolf. She had announced so very many tragedies over the past few years that I'd finally stopped believing them, or I didn't believe them very much. So when she told me she'd signed some papers I didn't pay a lot of attention or insist on more information. More than anything else, I was exhausted, her games had simply worn me out. Even if I had insisted, even if I had known about it sooner, it would have been useless, because she'd already signed those papers some time before without saying a word about them to me.

The real shock had come earlier, at the end of February, when I discovered that the papers Ilaria had signed made her the guarantor of her doctor's business to the tune of three hundred million lire. During those two months the company she'd signed the guaranty for had gone bankrupt, they were nearly two billion in the hole, and the banks had started calling in their loans. At this point your mother had come to me in tears, asking me what she could possibly do. The collateral she'd put up for the guaranty turned out to be the apartment where you both lived, that's what the banks wanted back. You can imagine how furious I was. Your mother was past thirty, and not only was she totally incapable of supporting herself, but she had gambled her sole possession, the apartment I signed over to her the day you were born. I was seething, but I didn't let her see it. To keep from upsetting her further I pretended to be calm and said, "Let's see what we can do."

Since she then withdrew into complete apathy, I started looking for a good lawyer. I spontaneously became a detective and collected all the information we'd need to win our case against the banks. While doing this I came to find out that her doctor had been giving her powerful mind-affecting drugs for many years. If she was a bit down during one of their sessions, he'd offer her whiskey. He never stopped repeating that she was his favorite, his most gifted pupil, and that soon she'd be able to set up a practice and have patients of her own. Just repeating those words gives me the shivers. Picture Ilaria, of all people, so fragile, so confused, so utterly centerless, taking on patients! That's what would have happened, almost certainly, if that company hadn't folded: without telling me anything, she would have started practicing the same arts as her guru.

Naturally she would never have dared tell me about this project of hers in any explicit way. Whenever I asked her why she didn't put her literature degree to some use, she'd reply with a knowing little smile, "You'll see, I'll put it to use . . ."

It's very painful to think about some things, talking about them is even harder. During those impossible months I understood one thing about her, something that had never entered my mind before, and I don't know if I'm doing right to mention it; however, seeing that I've decided not to hide anything from you, I may as well go on. So. What I had suddenly understood about your mother was that, well, she wasn't intelligent at all. The process I went through to understand this and then accept it was extremely difficult, partly because we always deceive ourselves about our own children, and partly because she had succeeded in throwing up quite a smokescreen with her feigned knowledge and her dialectical method. If I'd had the courage to face the truth before it was too late, I would have protected her better, I would have loved her more firmly. Maybe, if I had protected her, I could have saved her.

This was the most important thing, but by the time I became aware of that there was practically nothing to be done. Considering the situation as a whole, at that point there was only one possible course of action, namely to declare her mentally incompetent and institute proceedings for undue influence. The day I told her that the lawyer and I had decided to take this approach, your mother went into hysterics. "You're doing this on purpose!" she kept shouting. "It's all a plot to take the child away from me!" Nevertheless I'm sure that what was bothering her the most deep down inside was the thought that being declared incompetent would mean her career was permanently over before it started. She was walking blindfolded on the edge of a chasm and she still believed she was out picnicking in a meadow. Then she ordered me to drop the lawyer and forget the whole thing. She consulted another lawyer on her own, and I heard no more on the subject until the day she brought me the forget-me-nots.

Can you understand how I felt when she braced her elbows against the table and asked me for money? Yes, of course I know I'm talking about your mother and maybe you can't find anything but hollow cruelty in my words, maybe you think she was right to hate me. But remember what I told you to begin with, your mother was my daughter, I lost much more than you did. You're innocent of her loss, but I'm not, not at all. If every now and then it seems to you that I talk about this in a detached way, try to imagine how great my grief is, how indescribable in words. The detachment is only apparent, it's the vacuum that enables me to keep on talking.

When she asked me to pay her debts, for the first time in my life I told her no, unequivocally no. "I'm not a Swiss bank," I said. "I don't have that kind of money. And even if I did I wouldn't give it to you, you're old enough to be responsible for your own actions. The only property I had was that apartment and I signed it over to you. If you've lost it, that's got nothing to do with me." She started sniveling at this point. She'd start a sentence, stop halfway through it and start another; I couldn't make any sense or see any logic in what she was saying. After ten minutes' worth of whining she arrived at her favorite theme: her father and the wrongs he had supposedly done her, chief of which was that he hadn't paid her much attention. "I want compensation, you understand?" she yelled at me with a terrible glitter in her eyes. And then I just exploded. The secret I'd sworn to carry to my grave rose to my lips. I was sorry as soon as I'd spoken it, I wanted to take it back, I would have done anything to swallow those words, but it was too late. That "Your father wasn't your real father" had already reached her ears. Her face got even paler than before. She rose slowly to her feet, staring at me all the while. "What did you say?" Her voice was barely audible, but strangely enough I was calm again. "You heard right," I replied. "I said that my husband was not your father."

How did Ilaria react? She simply went away. Moving more like a robot than a human being, she turned and walked toward the garden gate. "Wait! Let's talk!" I shouted to her in a hatefully shrill voice.

Why didn't I get up, why didn't I run after her, why did I basically do nothing to stop her? Because my words had petrified me, too. Try to understand: what I had guarded so carefully for so many years was now out. In less than a second, like a canary who suddenly finds the door of his cage ajar, it had flown away, and to the one person I didn't want it to reach.

That very afternoon, around six, while I was watering the hydrangeas, still in a daze, some highway patrolmen came to inform me of the accident.

Now it's late in the evening, I had to take a break. I fed Buck and the blackbird, I had a bite myself, I watched a little television. My shredded old shell won't let me bear strong emotions for very long. If I want to keep on going I have to distract myself, catch my breath.

As you know, your mother didn't die right away, she hovered between life and death for ten days. I was by her side the whole time, I was hoping she'd open her eyes if only for a moment and give me one last chance to beg her pardon. We were alone in a little room full of machines, one small television showed that her heart was still going, another that her brain had almost stopped. The doctor who was caring for her had told me that patients in that state can sometimes benefit from hearing sounds they've loved, so I got hold of a cassette with the song that was her childhood favorite and played it to her for hours on a little tape machine. Something must actually have reached her, because the expression on her face changed at the very first notes, her features relaxed and she began to move her lips the way nursing infants do after they've eaten. It seemed like a smile of satisfaction. Who knows, maybe the memory of some happy time was stored in the small portion of her brain that was still working and she had taken momentary refuge there. That tiny alteration filled me with joy. At such times you grasp for straws. I kept stroking her head, kept repeating over and over again, "Darling, you've got to make it, we still have a whole lifetime of living together in front of us, we'll start all over again, everything will be different." While I was talking to her, an image kept appearing before my eyes: she was four or five years old, and I saw her wandering around the garden, holding her favorite doll by the arm, talking to it nonstop. I was in the kitchen, I didn't hear her voice. Every now and then I could hear her laughing, a hearty, joyous laugh. If she was happy once, I told myself, she can be happy again. And her rebirth has to start from there, from that child.

Naturally, the first thing the doctors told me after the accident was that even if she survived she'd never be the same, she might be paralyzed or have permanent brain damage. And do you know, in my maternal selfishness the only thing I cared about was that she should stay alive, it didn't matter in what state. Indeed, pushing her wheelchair, washing her, spoonfeeding her, looking after her as my life's sole purpose—that would be the best way to expiate my guilt. If my love had been genuine, if I had loved her with all my heart, I would have prayed for her death. But in the end Someone loved her more than I did: late in the afternoon of the ninth day, that vague smile disappeared from her face and she died. I realized it at once, I was there beside her, but I didn't tell the nurse on duty right away because I wanted to stay with her a little longer. I caressed her face, I squeezed her hands the way I used to do when she was a child, I kept repeating, "Darling, darling." Then, without letting go her hand, I knelt by the bed and began to pray. And as I prayed, I began to cry.

I was still crying when the nurse touched my shoulder. "Come with me," she said, "I'll give you something to calm you." I didn't want to be calm, I didn't want anything to dull my grief. I stayed there until they took her to the funeral home. Then I took a taxi to the friend's house where you were, and by evening you were home with me. "Where's Mama?" you asked me during dinner. "Mama's gone away," I told you. "She's gone on a trip, a long trip right up into the sky." You continued eating in silence, I watched your big blond head. As soon as you had finished, you asked me in a serious voice, "Can we wave to her, Grandma?" "Of course, my love," I replied, picked you up in my arms, and carried you out into the garden. We stood on the lawn for a long time while you waved your little hand at the stars.

December 1

I'VE BEEN in a terrible mood these last few days. It's not due to anything in particular, the body's like that, it has its own internal balances, it doesn't take much to throw them off. Yesterday morning, when Mrs. Razman came with the groceries and saw my long face, she said that in her opinion the moon was to blame. In fact, there had been a full moon the night before. And if the moon can affect the tides and make the radicchio in the vegetable garden grow faster, why shouldn't it have power over our moods as well? What are we made of if not water, gas, and minerals? Anyway, before she went away she left me an impressive stack of trashy magazines, and so I've spent the entire day reading myself into stupidity. I get taken in every time! When I first see them I tell myself, All right, I'll flip through them for half an hour, no more, and then I'll go do something more worthwhile. But every time I hang on until I've read the very last word. The Princess of Monaco's unhappy life makes me sad; her sister's proletarian love affairs make me indignant; every tear-jerking sob story, recounted in such excruciating detail, makes my heart beat faster. And the letters! I never cease to be amazed by what people have the nerve to put in writing. I'm not an old prude—at least I don't think I am—but I won't deny that certain liberties leave me rather perplexed.

The temperature's gone down today. I didn't go for my walk in the garden, I was afraid the stiff wind would join forces with the chill I carry around inside and snap me in half like an old frozen branch. I wonder if you're still reading this. Now that you know me better, maybe you're so repulsed you can't go on. But the sense of urgency I feel at this moment doesn't allow me any loopholes, I can't stop or dodge away right now. Even though that secret has stayed inside me for so many years, I can't keep it any longer. I told you, when I first saw how bewildered you were because your life seemed to have no center, I was bewildered too, perhaps even more than you. I know your notions about your "center"—or rather about your lack of one—are inextricably linked to the fact that you've never known who your father was. Naturally, I had the sad duty of telling you where your mother had gone, and naturally, too, I was never able to answer your questions about your father. How could I? I didn't have the slightest idea who he was. One summer Ilaria went to Turkey by herself for a long vacation; when she came back from that vacation, she was pregnant. She was already past thirty, and a strange frenzy comes over women of that age who don't yet have children. Whatever it takes, they want a child, it makes no difference how or with whom.

And besides, at that time almost all women were feminists. Your mother and some of her friends had founded a club. Many things they said were valid, they were things I agreed with, but mixed in with those were many forced conclusions and distorted, unhealthy ideas. One of these was that women should have complete control over their bodies, and that having a child or not was solely up to them. The man was just a biological necessity and should be used as such. Your mother wasn't the only one who behaved like this; two or three of her friends had children in the same way. You know, it's understandable. The ability to give life makes you feel a sense of omnipotence. Death, darkness, the precariousness of existence—all these things recede into the background, you're putting another part of yourself into the world, and this miracle cancels out everything else.

Your mother and her friends found support for their ideas in the animal kingdom. They said, "The only contact that females have with males is when they mate. Then they go their separate ways and the young remain with the mother." I don't have any way of proving whether this is true or not. But I do know that we're human beings, every one of us is born with a face different from everyone else's, and that's the face we carry with us for life. Everything's in the face. There's your own history, there's your father, your mother, your grandparents and great-grandparents, maybe even a distant uncle nobody remembers anymore. Behind the face there's the personality, the good things and the not-so-good things passed on to you by your ancestors. The face is our first identity, it's what allows us to take our place in life and say, Look, here I am. So when you were thirteen or fourteen and began to spend entire hours in front of the mirror, I understood just what you were looking for. Sure, you were inspecting pimples and blackheads and that nose which suddenly seemed too big, but there was something else besides. You were looking past the features you got from your mother's side of the family and trying to picture the face of the man who fathered you. This was

December 1

just what your mother and her friends hadn't thought about enough: that one day the child would look in the mirror, realize there was someone else inside her, and want to know everything about that person. Some people spend their whole lives in pursuit of their own mother's or father's face.

Ilaria believed that genetics had practically no effect on a child's development. For her the important factors were education, environment, upbringing. I didn't share her ideas. As far as I'm concerned, there are two equally important parts in the equation: external influences count for half, and the other half is whatever we carry inside of us from birth.

Before you went to school I had no problem. You never asked questions about your father, and I was careful to avoid the subject. But as soon as you started grammar school, thanks to your little friends and those beastly themes your teachers assigned, you suddenly realized there was something missing in your everyday life. Naturally, lots of children in your class came from broken homes or unconventional situations, but no one except you had a complete blank for a father. You were six or seven years old. How could I explain to you what your mother had done? And besides, I didn't know anything at all aside from the fact that you were conceived in Turkey. And so, by way of inventing a story that wasn't completely incredible, I made use of the one fact I knew, your country of origin.

I had bought a book of Oriental fables, and I would read you one every night. Using them as a model, I made up a story especially for you. Do you still remember it? Your mother was a princess, and your father was a prince of the Crescent Moon. Like all princes and princesses, they were so much in love that each was prepared to die for the other. Many of the courtiers, however, were jealous of their love. The most jealous of all was the Grand Vizier, an evil, powerful man who cast a terrible spell on the princess and the child she was carrying in her womb. Fortunately, a faithful servant had warned the prince, and so one night your mother disguised herself as a peasant woman, left the castle, and took refuge here, in the city where you were born.

"I'm a prince's daughter?" you would ask me with shining eyes. "Of course," I would reply, "but it's a deep deep secret, and you must never tell anyone." What did I hope to accomplish with this bizarre lie? Nothing really, maybe just to give you a few more untroubled years. I knew one day you'd stop believing my stupid fairy tale. And I also knew that on that day you'd most probably start hating me. Nevertheless, it was absolutely impossible for me not to tell you that story. Even if I could have gathered together all my meager courage, I'd never have been able to say, "I don't know who your father was; maybe your mother herself didn't even know."

Those were the years of sexual liberation; erotic activity was considered a normal bodily function, to be indulged in whenever you felt like it, one day with one partner, the next day with another. Your mother had dozens of boyfriends—I don't remember a single one who lasted more than a month. Ilaria was already unstable by nature, and she couldn't deal with this amorous uncertainty the way others could. Although I never stopped her from doing anything or ever criticized her in any way, I was rather troubled by all this sudden permissiveness. It wasn't so much the promiscuity that shocked me, it was the way feelings became so impoverished. Once nothing was forbidden anymore and the sense of personal uniqueness was gone, passion went away too. Ilaria and her friends seemed to me like guests at a banquet suffering from bad colds and politely eating whatever was offered, but without being able to taste anything: carrots, roast beef, sweets, it was all the same to them.

The new sexual permissiveness certainly had a lot to do with your mother's choice, but maybe another factor was involved as well. How much do we know about how the mind works? A great deal, but not everything. Who can say whether she might not have had, in some obscure part of her consciousness, an intuition that the man she lived with was not her father? And might this not explain a lot of her anxieties and instability? I never asked myself these questions while she was little, nor when she was an adolescent and then a young woman; the fiction I let her grow up in was perfect. But when she came back from that trip with her three months' belly, then it all came home to me. You can't escape from falseness, from lies. Or rather, you can escape for a while, and then, when you least expect it, they spring up again, not so docile as they were when you told them, not so apparently harmless, no; while you thought they were far away they've transformed themselves into horrible monsters, all-consuming ogres. You uncover them, and a second later you're flat on your back, they're so tremendously greedy they devour you and everything around you. When you were ten, you came home from school one day in tears. "Liar!" you said to me and immediately shut yourself up in your room. You had discovered that my fairy tale was a lie.

Liar could be the title of my autobiography. In all my life I've told only one lie.

With that lie I destroyed three lives.

December 4

THE BLACKBIRD is still here on the table in front of me. Her appetite's not so good today, she's staying put in her box, not chirping at me constantly, not even poking her head out anymore—I can barely see the feathers on her cap. This morning, despite the cold, I went to the nursery with the Razmans. I didn't make up my mind until the last minute, the temperature was low enough to discourage a bear, and besides there was a voice in some dark recess of my heart saying, Why should you care about planting more flowers? But while I was dialing the Razmans' number to beg off, I glanced out the window and saw how faded the garden looked and regretted my selfishness. Maybe I won't see another spring, but surely you'll see many more.

I feel so restless these days! When I'm not writing, I wander from room to room, but there's no place where I feel at peace. I can't do very much, and nothing I try brings me closer to a state of rest or helps me turn my thoughts away from my sad memories. The pain that was part of them comes back again, as intense and stinging as it was when they were new long ago.

I was telling you about myself, about my secret. But a story should begin at the beginning, and this one starts in the days of my young womanhood. I was still living in the rather abnormal isolation I'd grown up in. Back then, intelligence didn't rate a very high position among the attributes of a marriageable woman; it was customary for a wife to be an inert, adoring broodmare, nothing more. A woman who asked questions, a curious, active wife was the last thing a man wanted, and therefore when I was young I was very solitary indeed. To tell the truth, between the ages of eighteen and twenty—seeing that I was pretty and from a fairly well-to-do family—I was surrounded by hordes of suitors. But as soon as I showed I knew how to speak, as soon as I opened my heart and talked about what was on my mind, I found myself surrounded by empty space. Of course I could have kept quiet and pretended to be something I wasn't, but unfortunately—or luckily—part of my true self had survived my upbringing and that part refused to be denied.

As you know, I didn't continue my studies past high school because my father forbade me to. My hopes died hard, and they left me with a thirst for knowledge. If some young man declared that he was studying medicine I riddled him with questions, I wanted to know everything, and I did the same with the future engineers and the future lawyers. My behavior provoked a lot of consternation, I seemed more interested in a person's studies than in the person himself, and in fact that was probably the case. When I talked with my girlfriends from school, I had the feeling I belonged to a world light-years away from the one they lived in. The great divide between us was caused by feminine wiles. I had none at all, they had developed theirs to the utmost. Behind their façade of arrogance and self-confidence, men are extremely fragile and ingenuous; they come equipped with some mighty primitive levers, all you have to do is pull one and its owner slides down into the skillet like a fish ready for frying. I caught on to this fact rather late, but my girlfriends knew all about it by the time they were fifteen or sixteen. They displayed a natural talent for accepting or rejecting the little notes sent to them, writing shrewdly calculated replies, making dates and not showing up —or showing up outrageously late. At dances they'd stroke certain parts of their bodies, and while stroking themselves they'd stare into the man's eyes with the stricken expression of young fawns. That's what I mean by feminine wiles, the little tricks that lead to success with men. But at that time, remember, I was like a potato, I didn't understand a thing that was going on around me. It may seem strange to you, but I had a deep sense of fair play, I knew I could never do anything so underhanded as to dupe a man. I thought that one day I'd find a young man I could talk to all night long without ever getting tired, and as we talked we'd realize we felt the same emotions and saw things the same way. Love would start to grow in us then, a love based on friendship and mutual esteem, not on cheap tricks.

I wanted a loving friendship with a man, the kind of relationship between equals that men often have with one another. It was this masculine attitude, I believe, that struck terror into my suitors' hearts. And so I slowly dwindled into the role usually reserved for homely girls. I had lots of friends, but these friendships were all one-way: all my friends wanted to do was to tell me about their love problems. One by one my former schoolmates got married. At one point in my life it seemed I didn't do anything except attend weddings. Girls my age were having babies and I was still the spinster auntie, I lived at home with my parents and was by now almost resigned to being unmarried forever. "What can you be thinking about?" my mother said. "Is it possible you don't like Tom, or Dick, or even Harry?" It was clear to my parents that my difficulties with the opposite sex were caused by my bizarre character. Was I sorry about that? I don't know.

Frankly, I didn't feel any burning desire to have a family. The idea of bringing a child into the world made me rather uneasy. I'd suffered too much as a child and I was afraid of causing an innocent creature to suffer in the same way. Besides, even though I still lived at home, I was completely independent, every hour of the day was my own. I earned a little money by tutoring students in Greek and Latin, my favorite subjects, but aside from this I had no obligations, I could spend entire afternoons in the public library without having to account to anyone for my time, I could take a trip to the mountains whenever I felt like it.

In fact, compared to other women I was living a life of freedom, and the thought of losing that freedom really scared me. And yet with the passage of time all my freedom, all my apparent happiness, began to feel more and more false and forced. Solitude, which I'd considered a privilege at first, started to weigh on me. My parents were getting old, my father had suffered a stroke and couldn't walk very well. Every day I'd take him by the arm and we'd go buy the newspaper—I must have been twenty-seven or twenty-eight then. As I watched our images reflected together in the shop windows, all at once I felt old too, and I realized the direction my life was taking: soon he'd die, before long my mother would follow him, and I'd be left alone in a big house filled with books. Maybe I'd take up embroidery to pass the time, or painting watercolors, and the years would fly away, one after the other. Finally, one morning someone who hadn't seen me for a few days would get worried and call the fire department, the firemen would break down my door, they'd find my body lying on the floor. I'd be dead, and what was left of me wouldn't be much different from the dry carcasses that insects leave on the ground when they die.

My woman's body was fading without ever having lived, and this made me feel very sad, not to mention completely alone. I had never in all my life had someone I could talk to, I mean really talk to. Certainly, I was very intelligent, I read a great deal; my father eventually came round to saying, with a certain amount of pride, "Olga won't ever get married, her head's too full of brains." But all this supposed intelligence was getting me nowhere, I wasn't capable of setting out on a long trip, say, or studying anything in depth. I felt hobbled because I didn't have a university education, but the real cause of my incompetence, of my inability to make use of my gifts, had nothing to do with education. After all, Schliemann was self-taught, and he discovered Troy. What was holding me back was something else: the little dead thing inside of me, remember? He was the obstacle, he was why I couldn't go forward. I stood still and waited. For what? I didn't have the slightest idea.

Snow had fallen the day Augusto came to our house for the first time. I remember it because snow falls rarely in those parts, and because it was the snow that caused our guest to arrive late for lunch. Augusto, like my father, was a coffee importer, and he had come to Trieste to discuss the sale of our business. Since my father had no male heirs, after his stroke he'd decided to sell the company and live out his last years in peace. My first impression of Augusto was that I didn't care for him at all. He came from Italy, as people from our part of the country used to say, and like all Italians he had his irritating affectations. It's strange, but it often happens that persons destined to play an important part in our lives rub us the wrong way at first sight. After lunch my father retired for his nap, and I was left to keep our guest company in the living room until it was time for his train. I was most annoyed. Every time he asked a question I answered with a monosyllable, and if he hushed up I hushed up too. When he left, he said, "Well, goodbye, miss," and I put out my hand to him like a haughty aristocrat condescending to someone of inferior rank.

"For an Italian, this Augusto is quite nice," my mother said at supper that evening. "He's a man of integrity," my father replied, "and a good businessman besides." Guess what happened then? My tongue took off on its own. "And doesn't have a wedding ring on his finger!" I cried out briskly. "True, poor man, he's a widower," my father answered, and I was so embarrassed with myself I turned red as a pepper.

Two days later, coming back from a tutoring session, I found a package wrapped in silver paper beside the front door. It was the first package I ever got in my life, I couldn't imagine who'd sent it to me. Inside there was a note: *Perhaps you've never tasted these?* It was signed Augusto.

That night, with those marzipan candies on my night table, I couldn't go to sleep. I told myself he'd sent them as a courtesy to my father, and meanwhile I was devouring one after the other. Three weeks later he came back to Trieste, "on business" was what he said during lunch, but this time he stayed in town awhile instead of leaving right away. Before he said goodbye he asked my father for permission to take me for a drive, my father granted it at once, I was not consulted. We drove through the streets of the city the whole afternoon; he spoke very little, he asked about the various monuments and then listened to my answers in silence. He listened to me; a true miracle, in my view.

The morning he left he sent me a bunch of red roses. My mother was all excited, I pretended not to be, but I waited several hours before I opened his note and read it. Within a short time he was making weekly visits; he'd come to Trieste every Saturday and return home every Sunday. Do you remember how the Little Prince went about taming the fox? Every day he went to its den and waited for it to come out. Thus, little by little, the fox got to know him and overcame its fear. Not only that; the fox reached the point where it started to get excited at the mere sight of anything that reminded it of its little friend. Seduced by the same kind of tactics, I found I was starting to get excited every Thursday: the process of taming me had begun. By the time a month had passed, my entire life revolved around waiting for the weekend. It hadn't taken long for a feeling of great intimacy to develop between us. At last there was someone I could talk to, someone who appreciated my intelligence and my desire for knowledge; for my part, I appreciated his calm demeanor, his willingness to listen, that sense of security and protection that older men can give to young women.

We were married in a simple ceremony on June 1, 1940. Ten days later Italy was at war. To be safe, my mother went to live in a small village in the Veneto mountains, while my husband and I went to L'Aquila, his hometown.

You've only read books about the history of those years, you didn't live through them, so it must seem strange to you that all those tragic events made so little impression on me. The Fascists were running the country, the racial laws were in force, war had broken out, and I continued to concern myself exclusively with my little personal difficulties, the microscopic movements of my spirit. But don't imagine that my attitude was exceptional, it was just the opposite. Outside of a small politicized minority, everyone in our city behaved like this. My father, for example, considered fascism pure buffoonery. At home he referred to the Duce as "that watermelon vendor." But then he'd go to dinner with the party officials and stay there talking to them until late in the night. In the same way, I found "Italian Saturdays" absolutely ridiculous and boring, all that marching around and singing and having to wear black like a widow, but I attended them all the same, I thought they were an annoyance you had to put up with if you wanted to live in peace. Not an heroic way to behave, but a very common one. A peaceful life is one of the great human ambitions, at least it was back then and probably still is today.

In L'Aquila we lived in Augusto's family home, a large apartment in a stately palazzo situated in the center of the city. All the furniture in the place was glum and heavy, the light was dim, the general aspect was just plain sinister. My heart sank as soon as I stepped inside. Is this where I have to live, I asked myself, with a man I've known for barely six months and in a city where I don't have a single friend? My husband perceived my dismay at once and during the first two weeks he did everything he could to distract me. Every other day he'd get the car out and we'd go for drives in the surrounding mountains. We both loved to go on excursions. The sight of those beautiful mountains and those solidly anchored hilltop villages—like something out of a Nativity scene—calmed me down a little; it was almost as if I'd never left my northern home. We still talked a great deal. Augusto loved nature, particularly insects, and as we hiked around he'd explain lots of things to me. Most of what I know about natural history I owe to him.

At the end of those two weeks, which had constituted our honeymoon, he went back to work and I began my new life, alone in that vast apartment. An old servant was there with me, she took care of most household chores. Like all middle-class wives, I was supposed to plan the lunch and dinner menus, but other than that I had nothing to do. I took to going out for long walks every day, alone. I'd rush up and down the streets at a furious pace, my head was teeming with thoughts, but they weren't much help in making sense of what was going on. I'd come to a sudden stop and ask myself, Do I love him, or has this all been a colossal blunder? When we were at the table or sitting in the living room in the evening, I'd look at him and ponder the question: What do I feel? I felt tenderness, that much was certain, and he surely felt the same for me. But was that love? Was that all? Since I'd never felt anything else, I couldn't give an answer.

After a month the first tattle reached my husband's ears. Anonymous voices reported that "the German woman goes walking around the streets alone at all hours of the day." I was dumbstruck. Customs were different where I'd grown up, I could never have imagined that innocent walks could cause a scandal. Augusto was not pleased, he understood that this problem was incomprehensible to me, yet for the sake of civic tranquility and his own good name he requested that I refrain from further solitary forays. Six months of living like that drained me completely. The little dead thing inside me had become a giant dead thing, I moved around like an automaton, my eyes were glazed. When I spoke, my words seemed distant, as if they were coming out of someone else's mouth.

Meanwhile I had met the wives of Augusto's colleagues, and every Thursday we'd meet in a café in the town center. Although we were all more or less the same age, they and I had exceedingly little to say to one another. We spoke the same language, but that was all we had in common.

Augusto was back in his element, and before long he started behaving the way men do in his part of the country. Soon we were eating our meals in virtual silence, he'd respond to my efforts at conversation with a monosyllabic yes or no. In the evenings after dinner he'd often go to his club, if he stayed home he'd close himself up in his study and rearrange his beetle collections. His great dream was to discover an insect no one had identified before so that his name would be passed on forever in scientific books and journals. I would have liked to pass on his name in another way, namely by having a baby; I was now thirty years old and I felt time slipping past me more and more swiftly. Things were going very badly in that area: there had been a rather disappointing first night, and not much had happened since. I got the feeling that what Augusto wanted more than anything else was to find someone at home during mealtimes, someone he could display with pride in the cathedral on Sundays; he seemed mostly indifferent to the living person behind that comforting image. What had happened to the pleasant, responsive suitor who courted me? Could it be possible that love was doomed to end up like this? Augusto had told me that male birds sing louder in the spring so that a female will be attracted by the song and thus persuaded to build a nest together with the singer. He'd done the very same thing, but once he got me in the nest he lost interest in my existence. I was there, I kept him warm, and that was it.

Did I hate him? No, you might think it strange, but I couldn't hate him. If you're going to hate someone, he has to wound you, he has to really do you wrong. Augusto never did anything to me, that was the trouble. You're more likely to die from nothing than from pain; you can rebel against pain, but not against nothing.

Naturally, whenever I spoke to my parents I said that everything was fine, I made a special effort to sound like a happy young bride. They were positive that they had put me in good hands, and I didn't want to undermine their confidence. My mother was still hiding out in the mountains, my father had stayed put in our family home, alone except for a distant cousin who was looking after him. We had a regular monthly ritual. "Any news?" he'd ask me, and I'd answer no, not yet. He was yearning for a grandchild, senility had brought him a tenderness he'd never had before. I felt closer to him now that he'd changed, and I didn't like disappointing him. At the same time, however, I didn't have the nerve to tell him the real reason behind my prolonged infertility. My mother wrote long letters clogged with rhetoric. My adored daughter, she'd put at the top of the page, and follow that with a meticulous list of all the insignificant occurrences that had made up her day. In closing, she'd inevitably announce that she'd finished knitting yet another little outfit for the grandchild on the way. In the meantime I was shriveling up, every morning I'd look in the mirror and find myself uglier than the day before. Sometimes in the evening I'd ask Augusto, "Why don't we talk?" "About what?" he'd reply, without lifting his eyes from the magnifying glass he was using to examine an insect. "I don't know," I'd say. "Maybe we could tell each other stories." At that point he'd shake his head. "Olga," he'd say, "you really have an overactive imagination."

It's a commonplace that a dog and his master, if they live together for a long time, will gradually begin to look like each other. I had the sensation that the same thing was happening to my husband, the more time passed the more he resembled a beetle. In every way. His movements didn't seem human anymore, they were geometrical instead of fluid, every gesture proceeded by a series of jerks. And his voice was toneless, a metallic sound that came from some vaguely defined area in his throat. He was obsessively interested in his insects and his work, but other than those two things there was nothing that stirred him even a little. Once he picked up a ghastly bug and showed it to me, I think he called it a mole cricket. "Look at those mandibles," he said. "With those he can eat anything at all." That night I dreamed about him in the same shape, but enormous, and he was devouring my wedding dress as if it were cardboard.

After a year we started sleeping in separate rooms, he liked to stay up late with his beetles and didn't want to disturb me, or at least so he said. Described this way, my marriage must seem extraordinarily awful to you, but in fact there was nothing extraordinary about it. In those days almost all marriages were like this, little domestic infernos for two, one of whom was bound to succumb sooner or later.

Why didn't I revolt, why didn't I pack my bags and go back to Trieste?

Because there wasn't any such thing as separation or divorce back then. The marriage bond could be broken only in cases of severe mistreatment, otherwise a woman needed to be rebellious enough to take flight and spend the rest of her days as a wandering fugitive. But rebellion, as you know, isn't part of my character, and Augusto never even raised his voice to me, let alone his hand. He made sure I never lacked for anything. After mass on Sundays we'd stop at the pastry shop and he'd let me buy whatever struck my fancy. It won't be hard for you to imagine how I felt every morning when I woke up. After three years of marriage the only thought in my mind was the thought of death.

Augusto never talked to me about his first wife, on the few occasions when I made discreet inquiries he changed the subject. Time went by, and as I wandered through those spectral rooms on winter afternoons I convinced myself that Ada (that was her name) hadn't died of a disease or in an accident, but by her own hand. When the servant was out I spent my time unscrewing boards, going through drawers, feverishly seeking some trace or sign that would confirm my suspicions. One rainy day I found some women's clothes—hers—at the bottom of a wardrobe. I pulled out a dark dress and put it on; we wore the same size. As I looked at myself in the mirror, I began to cry. I cried silently, without sobbing, like someone who knows her fate's already sealed. In one obscure room there was a heavy wooden prie-dieu that had belonged to Augusto's mother, a very devout woman. Whenever I didn't know what to do I'd shut myself up in that room and kneel there for hours with my hands clasped. Was I praying? I don't know. I was talking or trying to talk to Someone who I supposed was located somewhere above my head. I'd say, Lord, let me find my way, if this is my way help me to bear it. Habitual church attendance—a habit demanded by the married state—had resurrected questions buried in my mind since childhood. The incense dazed me, and so did the organ music. As I listened to the Holy Scriptures, something inside me vibrated weakly. However, when I ran into the priest on the street, without his sacred vestments, when I looked at his spongy nose and piggy eyes, when I listened to his banal, irredeemably false questions, all vibrating ceased, and I told myself, See, it's nothing but a hoax, a way to help the weak-minded endure the oppression of their daily lives. All of which notwithstanding, I loved to read the Gospels in that silent house. I found many of Jesus' words extraordinary, they made me feel so fervent I'd repeat them aloud again and again.

My own family was not in the least religious, my father considered himself a freethinker, and my mother, whose family had been converted two generations ago, as I mentioned before—well, her attendance at mass was due to social conformity, pure and simple. On the rare occasions when I questioned her about religious matters, she answered, "I don't know, our family has no religion." No religion. That phrase weighed like a boulder on the most delicate phase of my childhood, when I was asking the biggest questions. Those words were like a mark of infamy, we had abandoned one religion in order to embrace another that we didn't have the slightest respect for. We were traitors, and for traitors there was no place anywhere, neither in heaven nor on earth.

So the few stories I'd learned from the sisters constituted all my knowledge of religion until I was thirty years old. The kingdom of God is within you, I'd repeat to myself as I wandered around the empty house. I'd try to imagine exactly where that might be: my eye would turn inward and descend inside me like a periscope, scrutinizing my body's innermost recesses and my mind's most mysterious depths. Where was the kingdom of God? I couldn't see it, there was heavy fog around my heart, not the luminous green hills I imagined in Paradise. In lucid moments I'd tell myself I was going crazy, like all old maids and widows, I was falling slowly, imperceptibly, into mystical delirium. After four years of this, it was becoming more and more difficult for me to distinguish between what was real and what was false. The bells in the nearby cathedral struck every quarter of an hour, I stuck cotton in my ears so I wouldn't hear them, or so I'd hear them less.

I had become obsessed with the notion that Augusto's insects weren't really dead; at night I'd hear their little feet scuttling through the apartment, they were scampering everywhere, climbing up the wallpaper, squeaking across the kitchen tiles, rustling over the living-room rugs. I'd lie in bed and hold my breath, just waiting for them to start creeping under the door and into my bedroom. I tried to hide my state from Augusto. In the morning, with a smile on my lips, I'd tell him what we were going to have for lunch and keep smiling until he went out the door. When he came home I welcomed him with the same mechanical smile.

The war, like my marriage, was in its fifth year, in February bombs had fallen on Trieste. During the bombers' final run my childhood home had been completely destroyed. The only casualty was my father's carriage horse—they found him in the garden with two of his legs blown off.

There wasn't any television then and news traveled more slowly. I found out we'd lost the house the following day, when my father phoned me. As soon as I heard his voice, I knew something serious had happened, he sounded like someone who'd stopped living some time ago. I felt really lost now, without a place of my own to go back to. I drifted through the house in a trance for two or three days. Nothing could shake me out of this torpor, I saw my years stretching out in front of me in a single continuous sequence, monotonous, colorless, uniform, one after the other until the day I died.

Do you know what's one mistake we always make? Believing that life's immutable, that once you get on a particular track you have to follow it to the end of the line. But it appears that fate has more imagination than we do. Just when you think you're in a situation you can't escape from, when you've reached the lowest depths of total desperation, everything changes as fast as a gust of wind, everything's overturned, from one second to the next you find you're living a new life.

Two months after the house was bombed the war was over. I went to Trieste immediately, my father and mother had already moved into a temporary apartment with some other people. There were so many practical things to be done that after only a week I'd almost forgotten about the years in L'Aquila. A month later Augusto came too. He had to take over running the business he'd bought from my father, he'd neglected it all during the war years and left it to be managed by others. And there were my parents, now homeless and getting really old. With surprising speed, Augusto decided to leave his hometown and move to Trieste; he bought this little house and garden on the high plateau above the city and by autumn we had all come here to live together.

Contrary to all prognostications, my mother was the first to go, she died in early summer. The years of loneliness and fear in the mountain village had undermined her stubborn frame. Her death strongly revived my desire to have a child. I was sleeping in the same bed with Augusto again, but in spite of this little or nothing went on between us at night. I spent a lot of time sitting in the garden with my father. And it was he who said to me one sunny afternoon, "Hot springs can do wonders for the liver—and for women."

Two weeks later Augusto put me on the train for Venice. There I took another train to Bologna, changed again, and arrived in Porretta Terme in the early evening. To tell the truth, I didn't have much faith in hot springs, I'd decided to go there mostly because I had a great desire for solitude, I felt a need for my own company, but not as I'd been in recent years. I had suffered. Almost everything inside me was dead, it was like a burned field, all black and charred. Only rain, sun, and fresh air could give that tiny part of me that was still alive the energy to grow again.

December 10

SINCE YOU went away I don't read the papers anymore, you're not here to buy them and nobody else brings me any. I missed them in the beginning, but little by little I began to feel relieved. I thought of Isaac Bashevis Singer's father, who said that of all the habits of modern man, reading the daily newspapers is the worst. In the morning, precisely when the spirit is at its most receptive, they pour into it all the evil the world has produced during the previous day. In his time you could save yourself by ignoring the newspapers, but nowadays that's not enough, there's radio and television, all you have to do is turn them on for a second and the evil catches up with you, it gets under your skin.

That's what happened this morning. I had the regional news on while I was getting dressed, and I heard that the refugee convoys have received permission to cross the border. They've been waiting there for four days, they weren't allowed to go forward and they couldn't turn back. They're carrying old people, sick people, women with small children. The announcer said the first contingent has already reached the Red Cross camp and the refugees are being cared for there. I'm deeply disturbed by this war, it's so close to us and so primitive. Ever since it broke out it's been like a thorn stuck in my heart. I know that's a banal image, but its very banality corresponds to the way I feel. After the first year, my grief began to give way to indignation, I couldn't believe that no one would intervene and put a stop to this slaughter. Then I had to resign myself: there aren't any oil wells in that country, just mountains of solid rock. In time indignation has turned into rage, and that rage is still gnawing away at me like an obstinate woodworm.

It's ridiculous for someone my age still to be so affected by a war. After all, dozens and dozens of wars are being fought on earth every day, it's something I should be used to after eighty years, like a callus. As far back as I can remember, refugees and armies—whether victorious or shattered —have been making their way through the tall yellow grass of the Carso: first there were the infantry troop trains of the Great War, with the bombs exploding on the high plateau; then the processions of survivors from the Greek and Russian campaigns, the Nazi and Fascist bloodbaths, the sinkhole massacres; and now once again there's the sound of cannon fire along the border, this exodus of innocent people fleeing the Balkan slaughterhouse.

A few years ago I traveled by train from Trieste to Venice in the same compartment with a medium, a lady a little younger than me wearing a beret. Naturally I didn't know she was a medium until I gathered as much from her conversation with the woman next to her.

"You know," she said as we crossed the Carso plateau, "if I go for a walk in these parts I can hear the voices of all those who've died here, I can't take two steps without being deafened by them. They all howl terribly, and the younger they were when they died, the louder they scream." Then she explained to her neighbor that a violent act alters the atmosphere of a given place forever: the air becomes corroded and thick, and that very corrosion encourages further brutality. In short, if blood has been spilled somewhere, more will be spilled on top of that, and later more again. "The earth," the medium concluded, "is like a vampire, once it tastes blood it wants to taste it again, it wants fresh blood, it can't ever be satisfied."

For years I've asked myself whether the place where we happen to live is cursed; I'm still asking myself the same question, but I can't find the answer. Do you remember all the times we went up to Monrupino together? When the north wind was blowing we'd stay up there for hours, just looking at the landscape as though we were looking down from an airplane. We could see for miles in every direction, we'd have contests to determine who could identify certain peaks in the Dolomites or pick out Grado da Venezia first. Now that I can't go there physically anymore, I close my eyes to see that landscape.

Thanks to the magic of memory, everything appears before me and around me just as though I were standing on that mountain lookout again. Nothing's missing, not even the sound of the wind or the fragrance of the season I've chosen. I stand there, looking at the limestone columns eroded by time, the great barren tract where the tanks practice their maneuvers, the dark promontory of Istria half sunk in the blue sea, I look at all those things around me and ask myself for the thousandth time, is there a false note in all this harmony? If there is, where can it be?

I love this region and maybe it's this love of

mine that prevents me from resolving the question; the only thing I'm certain about is that the visible features of the landscape influence the character of everyone who lives here. If I'm often harsh or brusque, if you're the same way, that's because of the Carso, its erosion, its colors, the wind that batters it. If we'd been born, say, among the Umbrian hills, maybe we'd have turned out to be milder types, maybe exasperation wouldn't have played such a large part in our temperament.

In any case, some small curse seems to have operated today, because when I came into the kitchen this morning I found the blackbird lying dead among her rags. She'd been seeming unwell for the past two days, eating very little and often dozing off between mouthfuls. She must have died right before dawn, because when I picked her up her head swung back and forth as though some spring had broken inside her. She was light, fragile, cold. I stroked her for a while, then wrapped her up in a cloth, I wanted to give her a little warmth. Snow was falling thick and fast outside, I shut Buck up in a room and went out. I don't have enough energy for digging with a spade anymore, so I chose the flowerbed where the softest earth is. I made a little trench with my foot, laid the blackbird inside, and covered her up. Before I went back to the house I recited the prayer you and I always used to say when we buried our little birds: "Lord, receive this tiny life as you have received all the others."

Do you remember how many we took care of and tried to save when you were a little girl? After every windy day we'd find an injured bird, they were finches, tomtits, sparrows, blackbirds, one time even a crossbill. We did all we could to heal them, but our efforts were nearly always in vain and we'd find them dead without warning from one day to the next. And what a tragedy such days always were, no matter how often it had happened before it never failed to upset you. After the burial you'd wipe your nose and eyes on your hand and shut yourself in your room "to deal with it."

One day you asked me how we would go about finding your mama, heaven was so big it would be easy to get lost in it. I told you heaven was like a big hotel, everyone up there had a room and after death all the people who had loved one another on earth would find their loved ones again in that room and stay together forever. This explanation satisfied you for a while, but after your fourth or fifth goldfish died you brought up the subject again: "What happens if there isn't enough space to fit everybody?" "If there isn't enough space," I answered, "you have to close your eyes and say 'Room spread out' over and over again for a whole minute. Then all at once the room will get bigger."

Are these childish images still preserved in your memory, or has your shell banished them? I'd forgotten this story until today, I remembered it while I was burying the blackbird. Room spread out, what fine magic! I'm sure your room must already be as crowded as the stands at a football game, what with your mother, the hamsters, the sparrows, and the goldfish. Soon I'll be going there too, will you want me in your room or shall I have to rent one nearby? May I invite the first person I ever loved, may I finally introduce you to your grandfather?

What did I think, what did I imagine that September evening when I got off the train at Porretta? Absolutely nothing. The smell of chestnuts was in the air and my first concern was to find the *pensione* where I'd reserved a room. At that time I was still very naive, I knew nothing about the ceaseless workings of destiny, if I had any conviction at all it was that things happened according to whether or not I made good use of my willpower. The moment I stepped onto the platform, my willpower evaporated, I didn't want anything, or rather only one thing: to be left in peace.

I met your grandfather on the very first evening, he and another person were dining at my *pensione*. Aside from an older gentleman, they were the only other diners, and they were having a fervent discussion about politics. The tone of your grandfather's voice annoyed me right away. A couple of times during dinner I stared at him the way you do at someone who's getting on your nerves, so you can imagine my surprise the next day when I discovered he was the resort doctor! He asked me questions about the state of my health for ten minutes, then when I was undressing something very embarrassing happened, I began sweating as though I were exerting a great effort. While he was listening to my heart, he said, "My goodness, you're scared to death!" and burst out laughing in a most vexatious way. He'd barely started taking my blood pressure when the little column of mercury shot up to the top of the gauge. "Do you suffer from hypertension?" he asked me. I was furious at myself, I kept trying to tell myself there's nothing to be afraid of, he's only a doctor doing his job, it's not normal or dignified to be so agitated. But no matter how often I repeated those rational words, I couldn't manage to regain my calm. As I was leaving his office, he gave me a sheet of paper outlining my regimen and shook my hand. "Relax and take it easy," he said. "Otherwise the waters won't do you any good at all."

That same evening he came and sat at my table after dinner. By the following day we were already going on walks around the town and chatting together. That impetuous exuberance that had irritated me so much at first was now beginning to fascinate me. Everything he said was ardent, fervent, it was impossible to be near him without being warmed by his passionate talk, by the heat of his body.

Some time ago I read in a newspaper that according to the latest theories love is born not in the heart but in the nose. When two people meet and like each other, they start sending out little hormones whose name I don't remember, but these hormones enter through the nostrils and ascend to the brain, and there in some secret convolution they let loose the hurricane of desire. In short, the article concluded, feelings are nothing but invisible odors. What absurd nonsense! Anyone who's ever experienced true love, love of the overmastering, indescribable kind, knows that assertions like these represent just one more gauche attempt to belittle the workings of the heart. Of course, the way the person you love smells can be profoundly exciting; but that excitement has to come after some previous attraction quite a bit different from a mere odor.

When I was near Ernesto in those days, for the first time in my life I had the sensation that my body had no boundaries. I felt there was a kind of impalpable aura around me, it was as if my outline had expanded and was setting off vibrations every time I moved. You know how plants behave when you don't water them for days? The leaves become limp, instead of lifting themselves to the light they droop like a gloomy rabbit's ears. Well, my life during the preceding years had been like an unwatered plant, the night dews had given me just enough nourishment to survive but aside from that I was starving, I had enough strength to stay on my feet but that was all. If you water the plant just once, it will begin to revive, its leaves will draw themselves up. That's what happened to me that first week. One morning six days after my arrival I looked in the mirror and realized I was a different woman. My skin was smoother, my eyes were brighter, I began to sing as I got dressed, and I hadn't done that since I was a child.

Considering this story from the outside, you may naturally think there were some doubts, some uneasiness, some torment underneath all this euphoria. After all, I was a married woman, how could I accept the companionship of another man so lightheartedly? But the fact is there were no doubts, no misgivings, and not because I was particularly open-minded, but because I was experiencing something purely physical, something that concerned my body alone. I was like a puppy that finds a cozy den after days of wandering the cold winter streets: he doesn't ask questions, he just settles down and enjoys the warmth. Besides, I had a very low opinion of my womanly charms, so I never even imagined that a man could feel that way about me.

On the first Sunday, when I was walking to mass, Ernesto pulled up beside me in a car. He stuck his head out of the window and asked, "Where are you going?" and as soon as I told him he opened the door for me and said, "Believe me, God will like it better if you come for a nice walk in the woods instead of going to church." After many twists and turns, we came to the start of a path that disappeared among the chestnut trees. I wasn't wearing the right shoes for walking on uneven ground, I was stumbling at every second step. When Ernesto took my hand, it seemed like the most natural thing in the world. We walked a long way in silence. The scent of autumn was already in the air, the earth was damp, many trees bore yellow leaves, and the light passed through them in a haze of soft colors. Eventually we came to a clearing; an enormous chestnut tree stood right in the middle of it. I remembered my oak and went up to the tree, first I stroked it with my hand and then I laid my cheek against it. At once Ernesto rested his head next to mine. It was the first time our eyes had ever been so close.

The next day I didn't want to see him. Friendship was changing into something else, and I needed time to think. I wasn't a young girl anymore, I was a married woman with all the attendant responsibilities, he was married too and with a son to boot. I had already foreseen my entire life, right up into old age, the fact that something I hadn't counted on was bursting in upon me filled me with anxiety. I didn't know how to behave. Anything new is always scary at first, you have to get over your alarm before you can proceed. So one minute I'd be thinking, This is a lot of foolishness, this breaks all previous records, I've got to forget everything and blot out the little that's happened so far. And the next minute I'd tell myself that letting this go would be the greatest foolishness of all, because for the first time since I was a little girl I felt alive again, everything was vibrating around me, inside me, it seemed impossible to give all that up. But then I had a suspicion, naturally enough, the same suspicion all women have (or at least used to have): that he was playing a game with me, that he wanted a bit of amusement and nothing else. All these thoughts were whirling around in my head while I sat alone in my drab room in the *pensione*.

I couldn't fall asleep until four o'clock that night, I was too excited. The next morning, however, I wasn't tired at all, I started to sing as I was getting dressed; in those few hours a tremendous desire to live had been born in me. On the tenth day of my stay I sent Augusto a postcard: *Wonderful air, mediocre food. Let's hope for the best,* I wrote, and signed off with an affectionate kiss. I had spent the previous night with Ernesto.

In the course of that night I suddenly realized that there are many tiny windows between the body and the spirit. If they're open, emotions flow freely back and forth, but if they're partially closed, not much can filter through. Only love can fling them open all together, all at once, like a gust of wind.

We were never apart during the last week of my stay in Porretta, we went on long walks, we talked our throats dry. What a difference between Ernesto's conversation and Augusto's! He was all passion and enthusiasm, he could discuss the most difficult subjects with absolute simplicity. We often spoke about God, about the possibility that something existed beyond tangible reality. He had fought in the Resistance, more than once he had looked death in the face. The notion of some higher power had occurred to him in those moments, not because he was afraid but because his consciousness had seemed to expand, to grow in scope. "I can't take part in rituals," he told me. "I'll never set foot in a church and I'll never be able to believe in dogmas or stories invented by other men." We took the words out of each other's mouths, we thought the same things, said them in the same way, it seemed we'd known each other for years instead of only two weeks.

We had only a little time left, the last few nights we hardly slept at all, we'd doze off just long enough to regain our strength. Ernesto was fascinated by the idea of predestination. "In the life of every man," he said, "there's only one woman he can achieve a perfect union with, and in the life of every woman there's only one man with whom she can become complete." But few, very few, were destined to find one another. All the others were condemned to live in a state of chronic dissatisfaction, of perpetual longing. "How many meetings like ours can there be?" he said, speaking into the dark room. "One in ten thousand, one in a million, one in ten million?" One in ten million, that was it. All the other couples were the result of compromises, transitory epidermal attractions, physical affinities, similarities of character, social conventions. After these considerations he could only repeat, "We're so lucky, aren't we? Who knows what's behind it all? Who knows?"

On the day I left, as we waited for the train in the tiny station, he embraced me and whispered in my ear, "What previous life did we meet in?" "In many, so many," I replied, and I began to cry. Hidden in my purse I had an address for him in Ferrara.

There's no use describing how I felt during the long hours of my journey home, I was in too much turmoil, my feelings were all at war with one another. I knew well that I had to achieve a metamorphosis in the course of those hours, and I kept making trips to the toilets to check the expression on my face. The light in my eyes and the smile on my lips had to go. Only the color in my cheeks could remain, proof that the healthy air had been good for me. Both my father and Augusto found my improvement extraordinary. "I knew the waters could work miracles," my father repeated about a hundred times, while Augusto—I could hardly believe it—bombarded me with gallant little attentions.

When you too fall in love for the first time, you'll understand how various and funny its effects can be. As long as you're not in love, as long as your heart is free and your eyes are your own, not one of all the men you might possibly be attracted to will give you a minute of his time; then, the moment one particular person steals your heart and you couldn't care less about the others, they all start following you around, sweet-talking you, paying you court. That's caused by those windows I was talking about before, when they're open the body shines a great light on the spirit and the spirit does likewise for the body, they illuminate each other with a system of mirrors. Within a short time a kind of warm, golden halo takes shape around you, and that halo draws men the way honey draws bears. Augusto was no exception, and it may seem strange to you but I didn't find it hard to be nice to him. Of course, if he had just lived a little closer to the real world, if he'd been just a bit craftier, it wouldn't have taken him long to figure out what had happened. For the first time since we got married I found myself feeling grateful to his nauseating insects.

Did I think about Ernesto? Of course, that's practically all I did. But think is not exactly the right word. I did more than think about him, I existed for him, he existed in me, we were one single person in every gesture and every thought. When we parted, we agreed that I'd be the first to write; before he could write back I'd have to find a friend, a woman I could trust to receive his letters for me. I sent him the first letter on All Saints' Day. The period of time that followed was the most terrible in our whole relationship. Not even the greatest, most absolute love is exempt from doubt when the beloved is far away. Some mornings when it was still dark outside I'd open my eyes all at once and lie motionless, silent, next to Augusto. Those were the only moments when I didn't have to hide my feelings. I'd think over those three weeks. I'd ask myself, What if Ernesto is only a seducer, and when life at the spa gets boring he amuses himself with the first available woman? The more days passed without a letter from him, the more that suspicion transformed itself into certainty. So I told myself, All right, even if that's all it was, even if I acted like a naive little fool, it wasn't a negative experience, it wasn't totally useless. If I hadn't let myself go I would have grown old and died without ever knowing what a woman is capable of feeling. You see, I was trying to put up some kind of shield, to soften the blow somehow.

Augusto and my father both noticed that my humor had taken a turn for the worse. I'd fly into a rage over nothing; as soon as one of them entered a room I'd exit in a huff and go somewhere else, I needed to be alone. I kept going over those weeks we'd spent together again and again, I scrutinized them frenetically, minute by minute, trying to find some clue, some proof that would make up my mind once and for all. How long did this torture last? One and a half months, nearly two. The week before Christmas the letter finally arrived at my friend's house, five pages written in a big, expansive hand.

Suddenly I was in a good humor again. Winter flew away, and spring did too, while I was writing letters and waiting for replies. My mind was so fixed on Ernesto that my perception of time was altered, all my forces were concentrated on some imprecise future, on the moment when I'd be able to see him again.

His first letter moved me so deeply that all my

doubts about the feelings we shared vanished away. Ours was a great love, an exceedingly great love, and like all truly great loves it was in large part insulated from ordinary human experience. Maybe it will seem strange to you that the great distance between us didn't cause us any terrible suffering, though it wouldn't be exactly true to say we didn't suffer at all. Ernesto and I both suffered from the enforced separation, but other feelings were mixed in with the suffering, the pain of being apart took second place to the excitement of anticipating the time when we'd meet again. We were two married adults, we knew we couldn't expect things to go any differently. If all this had happened a couple of generations later, I probably wouldn't have waited so much as a month to ask Augusto for a separation, Ernesto would have done the same with his wife, and we'd have been living in the same house by Christmas. Would that have been better? I don't know. I have a lot of trouble getting rid of the notion that easy relationships trivialize love and shrink passionate intensity into fleeting infatuation.

Having a lover and managing to see him wasn't a simple matter in those days. It was easier for Ernesto, of course, since he was a doctor he could always invent a meeting, a conference, some urgent case, but for me, whose only occupation was housewifery, it was virtually impossible. I had to come up with some obligation, something that would let me be away from the house for a few hours or maybe even a few days without arousing suspicion. And so right before Easter I joined a club for amateur Latin enthusiasts. They held meetings every week and frequently went on cultural excursions. Knowing my passion for ancient languages, Augusto neither suspected anything nor made any complaints, he was glad to see me going back to something I'd always been interested in.

That year summer arrived in a flash. At the end of June, Ernesto left Ferrara to spend the season at the spa, as he did every year, and I went to the seaside with my father and my husband. During the following month I succeeded in convincing Augusto that I hadn't stopped wanting to have a baby. Early in the morning of August 31, wearing the same dress and carrying the same suitcase as the year before, I got in the car and he drove me to catch the train for Porretta. I was so excited I couldn't sit still the whole trip, I looked out the window at the same landscape I'd seen last year, but everything seemed different.

I stayed at the spa for three weeks, and in those three weeks I lived more, and more deeply, than in all the rest of my life. One day while Ernesto was at work I took a walk in the park, and I remember thinking how beautiful it would be to die at that very moment. It seems strange, but the greatest happiness, like the greatest unhappiness, always carries with it this contradictory desire. I had the sensation of having been under way for a long time, of having marched on bad roads through the woods for years and years; I'd had to hack my way through the underbrush in order to make any progress at all, and I hadn't taken in any of my surroundings except for what was directly in front of me; I hadn't known where I was going—there could have been a precipice ahead, a gorge, a big city, or a desert; then all at once the woods ended, I'd been climbing steadily without realizing it, and now suddenly there I was standing on top of a mountain. The sun had just risen, and before me other mountains, wrapped in tinted mist, descended to the horizon. Everything was a hazy blue, a light breeze skimmed the summit, the summit and my head, my head and the thoughts inside. Every now and then a sound rose up from down below, a dog barking, a church bell ringing. Everything was strangely weightless and intense at the same time. Inside and outside of me everything had become clear, there were no blurred edges, nothing blocking the light, I didn't want to climb down again, to go back into the woods; I wanted to dive into that blue mist and stay there forever, to leave life behind now that I'd reached its peak. I kept that thought in my mind until the moment when I saw Ernesto again that evening. During

December 10

dinner I lost my nerve and couldn't tell him, I was afraid he'd start laughing. It was only late that night, when he came to my room, when he wrapped his arms around me, that I put my lips close to his ear and whispered to him. I intended to tell him, "I want to die," but do you know what I said instead? "I want a baby."

When I left Porretta I knew I was pregnant. I think Ernesto knew it too, in the last few days he was troubled, confused, often silent. My reaction was completely different. My body had started changing the morning after I conceived, my breasts were suddenly fuller, firmer, my complexion had a brighter glow. It's really incredible how quickly the body adjusts to its new condition. That's the reason why I can say I knew exactly what had happened, even though I hadn't taken a pregnancy test and even though my stomach was still quite flat. Suddenly I felt radiant, my body was altering itself, it was beginning to expand, I could sense its power. I had never known a feeling like that before.

Graver thoughts didn't begin to assail me until I was alone on the train. As long as I was with Ernesto, I hadn't any doubt that I'd keep my baby: Augusto, my life in Trieste, people's gossip, all that had seemed very far away. Now, however, that whole world was getting closer, my pregnancy wasn't going to slow down, I had to make some swift decisions and once they were made stick to them forever. Paradoxically, I realized at once that having an abortion would be much more difficult than having the baby. An abortion would never have escaped Augusto's notice. How could I justify it in his eyes after so many years of insisting that I wanted a child? And besides, I had no desire for an abortion, that little creature growing inside me hadn't been a mistake, it wasn't something to be erased as soon as possible. It was the fulfillment of a desire, perhaps the greatest and most intense desire of my life.

When you love a man—when you love him completely, body and soul—nothing's more natural than wanting a baby. This isn't an intellectual desire, it's not a choice based on rational criteria. Before I met Ernesto I imagined I wanted a child, and I knew exactly why I wanted one and all the pros and cons of going through with it. It was, in short, a rational choice, I wanted a child because I had reached a certain age and I was very much alone, because I was a woman and women, if they produce nothing else, can at least produce children. Do you see? If I'd been buying a car I would have applied exactly the same criteria.

But that night when I told Ernesto, "I want a baby," it was something utterly different. That decision was contrary to all good sense, and yet good sense was powerless against it. And besides, it wasn't actually a decision, it was a frenzy, a wild craving for perpetual possession. I wanted Ernesto inside me, with me, near me forever. Now, you're probably horrified to read about the way I behaved, you're asking yourself why you never noticed I was hiding such a base, despicable side of my character. When I arrived at the Trieste station I did the only thing I could do, I got off the train in the guise of an affectionate wife passionately in love with her husband. Augusto was struck at once by the change in me, but instead of wondering why he just let himself get swept along.

After a month it was extremely plausible that the baby was his. The day I told him the results of the pregnancy test he left his office in the middle of the morning and spent the whole day with me planning changes in the house for the baby's arrival. As for my father, when I put my mouth close to his ear and yelled the news, he took my hands in his own dry ones and remained like that for a while, without moving, as his eyes became moist and red. For some time his deafness had kept him pretty isolated from the life around him, and his conversation consisted of a series of jolts, there'd be sudden gaps between phrases, or he'd go off on tangents and tell stories from the past that had nothing to do with what was being talked about. I don't know why, but instead of being touched by his tears I felt vaguely annoyed. As far as I was concerned they were rhetoric and nothing else. In any case, he didn't live to see his grand-daughter. He died painlessly in his sleep when I was in my sixth month. When I saw him laid out in the coffin I was struck by how shriveled and decrepit he looked. His face had the same expression as always, distant and neutral.

Naturally, I wrote to Ernesto as soon as I got the test results; his reply came back within ten days. I waited a few hours before opening the letter, I was extremely agitated, I was afraid it might contain something unpleasant. I only made up my mind to read it late that afternoon, I shut myself up in the rest room of a café so I could have some privacy. His words were placid and reasonable: "I don't know that this is the best thing to do," he said, "but if it's what you want I respect your decision."

Now that I'd surmounted all obstacles, I began peacefully awaiting motherhood. Did I feel like a monster? Was I one? I don't know. All during my pregnancy and for many years thereafter I was untroubled by doubts or remorse. How could I pretend to love a man while carrying in my belly the child of the man I really loved? Look, things are never that simple in reality, they're never black or white, they're all different colors, and all of those have different shades. It wasn't a chore for me to be gentle and affectionate to Augusto because I genuinely loved him. I loved him much differently from the way I loved Ernesto, not the way a woman loves a man, but the way a sister loves an older brother who's just a bit tiresome. If he'd been a bad person, everything would've been different, I'd never have dreamed of having a baby and living in the same house with him, but he was only predictable and stupefyingly methodical; apart from that, he was at bottom a good and gentle man. He was happy to have that child, and I was happy to give her to him. What reason could there have been for revealing my secret? If I had done so I'd have made three lives permanently unhappy. Or at least that's what I thought at the time. These days, when you can move around freely and make your own choices, what I did may seem truly dreadful, but back then the situation I found myself in was quite common, I'm not saying it happened to every married couple but it was by no means unusual for a married woman to conceive a child with a man who wasn't her husband. And what happened? The same thing that happened in my case: absolutely nothing. The child was born, it grew up on an equal footing with its brothers and sisters and became an adult without ever being troubled by the slightest suspicion. In those days the family rested on extremely solid foundations, it took more to destroy them than a single questionable child.

So things went the same way with your mother: from the moment she was born she was our daughter, mine and Augusto's. For me, the most important consideration was that Ilaria's birth was due to love, not chance, social conventions, or boredom; I thought this fact alone would cancel out every other problem. What a mistake that was!

For the first few years, however, everything proceeded naturally and smoothly. I lived for her, I was—or believed I was—a very affectionate, very attentive mother. From her very first summer I took up the annual habit of taking her to the Adriatic coast, where we'd spend the hottest months together. We'd rent a house, and every two or three weeks Augusto would come and pass the weekend with us.

It was on that beach that Ernesto saw his daughter for the first time. Naturally, he pretended to be a perfect stranger, when we went for a walk he'd walk close to us "by chance," or he'd sit under a beach umbrella a few paces away and —when Augusto wasn't there—watch us for hours on end while ostensibly reading a book or newspaper. In the evenings he'd write me long letters, recording the thoughts that had passed through his mind, the sentiments he'd felt for us, the things he'd seen. Meanwhile his wife had also had a baby, another son, and Ernesto had resigned his spa job and set up a private practice in Ferrara, his hometown. Except for those carefully arranged "chance" encounters, we never saw one another at all during Ilaria's first three years. She absorbed all my attention; I woke up every morning overjoyed at the thought that she was there, even if I wanted to I couldn't have concentrated on anything else.

Shortly before we parted at the end of my last stay at the spa, Ernesto and I had made a pact. "Every evening," he'd said, "at eleven o'clock sharp, wherever I am and whatever I'm doing, I'll go outside and look for Sirius in the sky. You do the same, and that way, even if we're very far apart, even if we haven't seen each other for ages and have no idea what's going on, our thoughts will meet up there, at least they'll be close to one another." We both went out onto the balcony of the *pensione* and from there he showed me Orion and its bright star Betelgeuse, and then he pointed to Sirius shining nearby, the brightest of them all.

December 12

A SUDDEN NOISE woke me up last night, it took me a while to realize it was the telephone. It had already rung several times before I managed to get out of bed, and as soon as I reached it, naturally, it stopped. I picked up the receiver anyway and said hello two or three times in a very sleepy voice. Instead of going back to bed I sat down in the armchair near the phone. Was it you? Who else could it have been? That noise, breaking the nocturnal silence of the house, had really upset me. I remembered a story a friend told me some years ago. Her husband had been in the hospital for a long time, but the visiting rules there were so strict she hadn't been able to be with him the day he died. Crushed by frustration and grief, she couldn't sleep that night, she was lying there in the dark when the telephone suddenly started ringing. She was quite surprised, she couldn't believe anyone would be calling to offer condolences at that hour. When she reached for the receiver she noticed something striking and strange, there was a halo of light shimmering around the telephone, but as soon as she said hello her surprise turned to terror. The voice on the other end of the line seemed to come from very far away and spoke with great difficulty. "Marta," it said through the static and background noise, "I wanted to say goodbye before I left . . ." It was her husband's voice. He paused, for an instant there was a sound like a strong wind, then the line went dead and there was nothing but silence.

At the time I excused my friend because she was under a lot of stress, but the idea that the dead would avail themselves of such modern communications technology seemed to me bizarre to say the least. Nonetheless, that story must have left its mark on me. Deep down inside, very very deep down inside, in the most childlike and magical part of me, maybe I too would like to receive a midnight phone call sometime from someone on the Other Side. I've buried my daughter, my husband, and the man I loved most in the world.

They're dead, they're no longer here, and yet I continue to behave as though I've survived a shipwreck. I'm safe, I've been washed up on an island by the tide, I don't know what's happened to my companions. They disappeared from sight when the boat capsized, maybe they've drowned—it's almost certain they have—but it's just possible they haven't. In any case, months and years have gone by and I'm still scrutinizing the neighboring islands, waiting for a puff of smoke, a signal, something to confirm my inkling that they're all still alive with me under the same sky.

A loud noise awakened me the night Ernesto died. Augusto turned on the light and called out, "Who is it?" There wasn't anyone in the room, everything was in its usual place. It was only the next morning, when I opened the wardrobe door, that I realized all the shelves had fallen down inside, all my stockings, scarves, and underwear were lying in a pile at the bottom.

Now I can say "the night Ernesto died." I didn't know it then, however. I had just received a letter from him; the idea that something had happened to him couldn't have been further from my mind. I just figured that dampness had rotted the braces holding up the shelves and excessive weight had made them collapse. Ilaria was now four years old, she'd just started nursery school, my life with her and Augusto had settled into a calm routine. That afternoon, after a meeting with my Latin club, I went into a café to write to Ernesto. The club was planning a conference in Mantua in two months, and this would be our long-awaited opportunity to see each other again. Before going home I posted the letter, and after a week had passed I started expecting his reply. I didn't hear from him during the following week, nor in the weeks after that. I'd never had to wait so long before. At first I thought the postal service had made some blunder, then I imagined he might be sick and unable to go to his office to pick up his mail. A month later I wrote him a short note, but there was still no reply. As the days passed I began to feel like a house with water seeping into its foundations. The water started off as no more than a thin, discreet trickle, barely licking at the concrete substructure, but then as time passed it got bigger, more impetuous, its pressure was battering the cement into sand; the house was still standing, everything looked normal, but I knew it wasn't true, even a tiny shove would be enough to bring the facade and all the rest crashing down, collapsing upon itself like a house of cards.

By the time I left to go to the conference I was a shadow of my former self. After putting in a brief appearance in Mantua I went straight on to Ferrara, and there I tried to discover what had happened. There wasn't anyone in Ernesto's office, I passed by it at different times but the shutters were always closed. On the second day I went to a library and asked to see the newspapers from the previous months, and there in a short paragraph I found the whole story. On his way home from visiting a patient one night, he'd lost control of his car and crashed into a large plane tree. He died almost immediately. The date and the time corresponded almost exactly to the collapse of my wardrobe shelves.

In the astrology section of one of those wretched magazines Mrs. Razman brings me every now and then I once read that Mars in the eighth house presides over violent deaths. According to the article, no one born under this particular planetary configuration is destined to die peacefully in his bed. I wonder if Ilaria and Ernesto were born when this sinister combination was shining in the sky. More than twenty years apart, both of them, father and daughter, departed this life in exactly the same way, by crashing a car into a tree.

I sank into a deep depression after Ernesto's death. I'd been shining with a bright light for the past several years, and all of a sudden I realized that it hadn't come from within me, it was just a reflection. The happiness, the love for life I'd felt never really belonged to me at all, I had only served as a mirror. Ernesto emanated light, and I reflected it. Once he disappeared, everything became dim again. The sight of Ilaria didn't make me happy anymore, it just irritated me, I was so shaken I went so far as to doubt that she was really Ernesto's daughter. This change didn't escape her notice, she picked up my rejection on her child's antennae and became willful and overbearing. From then on she was the young vine, bursting with life, and I was the old tree ready to be smothered. She scented my guilt like a bloodhound, she used it to climb higher. The house had become a little hell filled with shrieks and bickering.

To relieve me of that burden, Augusto hired a woman to take care of the child. He'd tried for a while to interest her in his insects, but after three or four attempts—all of which ended with her screaming "That's disgusting!"—he gave it up. Suddenly he was showing his age, he seemed more like his daughter's grandfather than her father, he was kind but distant to her. When I looked at myself in the mirror I saw that I too had aged a great deal, my features had taken on a hardness they'd never had before. Neglecting myself was one way of exhibiting the self-contempt I felt. Between Ilaria's school and the woman who looked after her, I now had a lot of free time. Restlessness impelled me to spend most of that time in constant motion, I'd take the car and drive up and down the Carso plateau in a kind of trance.

I took up again some of the religious books I

had read during my stay in L'Aquila. I was hoping to find some sort of answer in those pages. I'd walk about repeating to myself St. Augustine's words on the death of his mother: "Let us not be sorrowful for having lost her, but rather thankful for having had her."

A friend had me meet with her confessor two or three times, but I left those meetings feeling more disconsolate than before. He used cloying, sugary words to celebrate the power of faith, as if faith were an item you could pick up in any grocery store. I wasn't able to resign myself to the loss of Ernesto; my light was gone and I couldn't see to find the reason why. You see, when I met him, when we fell in love, I immediately convinced myself that everything was resolved, I was happy to be alive, happy for everything around me; I felt I'd arrived at the high point of my life, at the most stable point; I was certain that nothing and nobody could budge me from where I was. I had that kind of prideful self-assurance that people have when they think they understand everything. For years I'd been sure I'd come all this way under my own power, but in fact I hadn't taken a single unaided step. I tried to walk on my own but my ankles gave way, the steps I took were unsteady, like the steps a little baby or an old person takes. For a moment I thought about using some kind of crutch: religion, perhaps, or work. That idea didn't last very long. Almost at once I understood that this would just be one more mistake. At the age of forty there's no more room for blunders. If all at once you find yourself naked, you must have the courage to look in the mirror and see yourself as you are. I had to start all over. Right, but from where? From myself. Easier said than done. Where was I? Who was I? When was the last time I had been myself?

As I told you, I was driving back and forth across the plateau for whole afternoons at a time. Occasionally, when I sensed that solitude would make me feel even worse, I went down into the city and mingled with the crowds, walking up and down the most popular streets and looking for some sort of relief. It was as though I now had a job, I'd go out when Augusto went out and return when he was coming home. My doctor had told him that in certain cases of nervous exhaustion the desire for a great deal of movement was not uncommon. Since I wasn't suicidal, there wasn't any risk in letting me dash about here and there. The more dashing I did, according to him, the more likely I was to calm down eventually. Augusto accepted this explanation, I don't know whether he really believed it or he was just being lazy because he wanted a quiet life. In any case, I was grateful to him for staying out of my way, for not putting up any obstacles around my great restlessness.

The doctor was right about one thing, despite the fact that I was having a nervous breakdown I wasn't suicidal at all. It's strange, but that's the way it was, I didn't think for a minute about killing myself after Ernesto died, and don't you believe it was Ilaria who was holding me back. As I've told you, she didn't mean a thing to me at the time. It was rather a feeling I had somewhere deep down that my sudden loss wasn't—mustn't be, couldn't be—an end in itself. It had to mean something, but finding out its meaning was like scaling a gigantic wall. Was it there just so I could get over it? Probably so, but I couldn't imagine what might be on the other side or what I'd see when I reached the top.

One day while I was out driving I came to a place I'd never been before. There was a tiny church with a little cemetery around it, on all sides there were wooded hills, and on the top of one of these I could see something white, it looked like part of an ancient fortress. A little past the church there were two or three peasants' houses, chickens were running free and scratching about in the road, a black dog was barking. The road sign said Samatorza. Samatorza, the name sounded like solitude to me, just the place for gathering one's thoughts. I was near the beginning of a stony path; I started walking without wondering where it might lead. The sun was already going down, but the farther I went the less I felt like stopping, every now and then a jay screamed and made me jump. There was something calling me to go on, I didn't figure out what it was until I came to a clearing and saw an enormous, placid, majestic oak tree, standing there in the middle with its branches spread like arms ready to welcome me.

It sounds silly, but as soon as I saw it my heart began to beat in a different way, it wasn't beating so much as whirring; it seemed like a contented little animal, it used to beat that way only when I saw Ernesto. I sat down under the tree, I caressed it, I leaned my back and head against its trunk.

Gnōthi seauton—when I was a girl I wrote this on the first page of my Greek exercise book. The words stayed buried in my memory until they suddenly came back to me there underneath the oak tree: *Know thyself.* Air, breath.

December 16

SNOW FELL last night, when I woke up the whole garden was white. Buck was running around the lawn like a crazy thing, jumping, barking, picking up branches in his mouth and tossing them in the air. Later Mrs. Razman dropped in for a visit, we had a cup of coffee and she invited me to spend Christmas evening with them. "What do you do all day?" she asked me before she left. I shrugged. "Nothing," I answered. "I watch a little television, I do some thinking."

She never asks about you, she's careful to avoid the subject, but I can tell from her tone of voice that she considers you ungrateful. In the middle of a conversation she'll frequently say something like, "Young people are heartless, they don't have any respect anymore." I nod agreement in hopes that she'll stop right there, but secretly I'm convinced that the heart is the same as it's always been; there's simply less hypocrisy, that's all. Young people aren't naturally selfish, any more than old folks are naturally wise. Your age doesn't have anything to do with whether you're sensitive or shallow, it's a question of the path your life takes. I can't remember where, but not long ago I read an American Indian saying that goes, "Don't judge a man until you've walked three moons in his moccasins." I liked it so much I wrote it down on a pad by the phone so I wouldn't forget it. Seen from without, many people's lives seem erroneous, irrational, deranged. It's easy to misunderstand other people and their relationships if we view them from the outside. Only by looking deeper, only by walking three moons in their moccasins can we comprehend their motives, their feelings, what makes them act one way and not another. Understanding comes from humility, not from the pride of knowledge.

Maybe you'll put on my slippers after you read my story? I hope so, I hope you'll spend a long time shuffling from room to room, I hope you'll take quite a few turns in the garden, from the walnut tree to the cherry tree, from the cherry tree to the rose, from the rose to those nasty black pines at the edge of the lawn. I hope you'll do this, not because I'm begging for compassion or looking for some kind of posthumous absolution, but because it's necessary for you and for your future. If you want to go forward unencumbered by lies, understanding where you come from and what's gone before you is the first step.

I should have written this letter to your mother, but I'm writing it to you instead. If I hadn't written it at all, then my existence really would have been a failure. Everybody makes mistakes, but if you die without ever having understood them you've lived your life in vain. The things that happen to us aren't ever gratuitous ends in themselves; every encounter, every little event, has some meaning, self-knowledge comes from willingness to accept new circumstances, from the ability to change direction at any given moment and leave old skin behind the way lizards do when the seasons change.

If I hadn't remembered that phrase from my Greek copybook that day when I was nearly forty years old, if I hadn't drawn a line there and started all over again, I would have kept on making the same mistakes I'd made up to that moment. I might have taken another lover to drive Ernesto's memory out of my mind, and then another, and another after that; searching for a copy of him, trying my best to relive the past, I could have tried out dozens of lovers. None of them would have matched the original, and I would have continued on, more and more unsatisfied, maybe even becoming a ridiculous old fool and surrounding myself with young men. Or I could have tried hating Augusto, whose presence, after all, was part of the reason why it hadn't been possible for me to make more drastic decisions. You see? The easiest thing in the world to do when you don't want to look inside yourself is to find escape hatches. You can always make it someone else's fault, it takes a lot of courage to admit that the fault—or rather the responsibility—is yours alone. And yet, as I've said before, this is the only way to go forward. If life's a road we travel, it's uphill all the way.

At the age of forty I understood where I had to start from. Understanding where I should arrive was a long process, filled with obstacles but fascinating nevertheless. You know, the TV and newspapers are always talking about the proliferation of religious gurus, and they're full of stories about people who suddenly abandon everything and follow some holy man. It scares me to think about these self-appointed masters cropping up everywhere and preaching ways to find inner peace and universal harmony. They're distress signals sent out by the general bewilderment. In the background, and not all that far in the background, is the fact that we're coming to the end of a millennium; calendar dates may be pure convention but this one's intimidating all the same; everyone's expecting something tremendous to happen and they want to be ready. So they gather around gurus, sign up for courses in how to find themselves, and after a month they're swollen with the arrogance unique to prophets—false prophets. One more great big scary lie!

The only master that exists, the only one that's true and believable is your own conscience. To find it you have to stand in silence—alone and in silence—you have to stand on the naked earth, naked yourself and with nothing around you, as if you were already dead. You don't hear anything at first, the only thing you feel is terror, but then you begin to hear a voice, away in the background, far off, it's a calm voice and maybe its banality gets on your nerves to begin with. It's strange, but when you're expecting the greatest things it's the little ones that turn up. They're so little and so obvious you feel like shouting, "Wait a minute, that's *it?*" If life has any meaning, the voice will tell you, that meaning is death; that's the central thing and everything else just swirls around it. A fine discovery, you'll remark at this point, a fine, morbid discovery, even the lowest imbecile knows he has to die. That's true, we all know that with our minds, but knowing a fact with your mind is one thing, and knowing it with your heart is something else again. When your mother was in her most arrogant attacking mode, I'd say to her, "You're hurting my heart." She'd laugh and answer, "Don't be ridiculous. The heart is a muscle, if you don't strain it, it can't hurt."

Many a time when she was old enough to understand, I tried to talk to her and explain the course of events that led me to withdraw my attention from her. "It's true," I said, "there was a certain period in your childhood when I neglected you, I was seriously ill. If I had tried to take care of you during my illness, it might have been even worse. But now I'm well, and we can talk, discuss things, start all over." She wasn't interested. "Now *I'm* the one who's sick," she'd say, and refuse to say anything else. I was at last achieving serenity and she hated it, she did all she could to undermine it and drag me down into her little daily infernos. She'd decided that unhappiness was her natural state. She'd conceived an idea of her life, and she put herself behind barricades so that nothing could blur that idea. Rationally, of course, she said she wanted to be happy; but in fact deep down inside her she'd already closed off any possibility of change by the time she was sixteen or seventeen. While I was slowly opening up, moving into a different dimension, she was standing there immobile with her hands over her head waiting for things to fall on her. My new calmness irritated her, when she saw the New Testament on my night table she said, "What do you need consolation for?"

When Augusto died she didn't even want to go to his funeral. He'd been suffering from a fairly severe form of arteriosclerosis for the past few years, he'd wander around the house talking baby talk and she couldn't stand it. "What does the gentleman want?" she'd cry out as soon as he shambled into whatever room she was in. She was sixteen when he passed away; she hadn't called him "Daddy" since she was fourteen. He died in the hospital one November afternoon. He'd been admitted the previous day because he'd had a heart attack. I was in the room with him, instead of pajamas he was wearing a white hospital gown with laces at the back. According to the doctors, the worst was over.

The nurse had just brought his dinner when he suddenly got out of bed and took a few steps toward the window, as if he had seen something. "Ilaria's hands," he said, glassy-eyed. "No one else in the family has hands like hers." Then he got back in his bed and died. I looked out of the window. A thin rain was falling. I stroked his head.

For sixteen years, without ever so much as dropping a hint about it, he'd kept that secret to himself.

December 16

* * *

It's noon, the sun's out and the snow's melting. I can see swatches of yellow grass on the lawn in front of the house, one after another drops of water are dripping from the branches of the trees. It's strange, but when Augusto died I became aware that death, in and of itself, doesn't always cause the same kind of grief. There's a sudden emptiness—the emptiness is always the same—but it's precisely within that emptiness that the different kinds of grief take shape. Everything we didn't say materializes and expands, expands and keeps on expanding. It's an emptiness without doors or windows, there's no way out; whatever's suspended in that void stays there forever, above your head, with you, around you, it envelops and confounds you like a thick fog. The fact that Augusto had known about Ilaria depressed me profoundly. At that point I would have liked to talk to him about Ernesto, about what he'd meant to me, I would've liked to talk to him about Ilaria; there were so many things I would have liked to discuss with him but by then it was too late.

Now maybe you can understand what I told you to begin with: the absence of the dead doesn't weigh so heavily on us as the burden of what was left unsaid between us and them when they died.

As I had done after Ernesto's death, after Augusto died I sought comfort in religion. I'd recently made the acquaintance of a German Jesuit just a few years older than me. Having noticed that religious services made me uneasy, after our first few encounters he suggested that we meet somewhere besides the church.

Since we both loved to go on walks, we decided to walk together. He came to get me every Wednesday afternoon with hiking shoes on his feet and an old knapsack on his back; I really liked his face, he had the hollow-cheeked grave face of a man born and raised in the mountains. In the beginning his being a priest made me feel shy, I left out half of every story I told him, I was afraid of scandalizing him or subjecting myself to rebukes and stern judgments. Then one day while we were resting, sitting on a rock, he said, "You're hurting yourself, you know. Only yourself." From that moment I stopped lying, I opened my heart to him as I'd opened it to no one else since Ernesto died. I talked and talked; pretty soon I forgot I had a man of the cloth in front of me. Unlike the other priests I'd met, he didn't seem to know any words of condemnation, or of consolation either, for that matter; he didn't deal in cheap sugarcoated messages. He had an unyielding quality that could seem off-putting at first sight. "Only pain makes us grow," he said. "But pain has to be met head on, whoever dodges or feels sorry for himself is bound to lose."

Winning, losing, the military terms he used helped to convey his image of a silent, completely interior struggle. According to him the human heart was like the earth, half lit by the sun and half in shadow. Not even the saints were all light. "Because of the simple fact that we have bodies," he said, "part of us remains in shadow, we're like frogs, we're amphibious, part of us lives down here and the other part is always yearning upward. Living is only being conscious of this, knowing it, and struggling to prevent the dark shadow from eclipsing the light. Don't trust people who are perfect, those who have all the answers ready to hand. Don't trust anything except what your heart tells you." His talk fascinated me, I'd never met anyone who expressed so well the feelings that had seethed in me for years without ever finding a vent. My thoughts took shape as he spoke, all at once I could see my road in front of me; traveling it no longer seemed impossible.

Occasionally his knapsack contained some book particularly dear to him; during our rest stops he'd read me passages in his clear, stern voice. Through him I discovered the prayers of the Russian monks, the oration of the heart, I understood parts of the Gospels and the Old Testament that had seemed obscure to me up to then. During the years that had passed since Ernesto died I had indeed made an interior journey, but it was a journey limited to self-knowledge. At a certain point I'd found myself standing in front of a wall, I knew that the road went on broader and brighter on the other side of that wall, but I didn't know how to go about climbing over it. One day, during a sudden shower, we took shelter in the entrance of a cave, and there I asked him, "What does a person have to do to acquire faith?"

"You don't *do* anything, it comes to you," he replied. "You've got it already, but your pride won't let you admit it, you pose too many questions, you make simple things too complex. The fact is, you're just tremendously scared. Let yourself go, and what must come will come."

I always got back home from those walks more confused and uncertain than before. He could be disagreeable, as I've said, and his words wounded me. Quite a few times I resolved never to see him again, Tuesday evening would come and I'd say to myself, Now I'm going to phone him and tell him not to come tomorrow because I'm not well, but I never actually put a call through. Wednesday afternoon would find me waiting punctually at my door, carrying a knapsack and wearing my hiking shoes.

Our excursions lasted a little more than a year, then one day without warning his superiors changed his assignment.

What I've told you may make you think that

Father Thomas was an arrogant man, that there was vehemence or fanaticism in his words, in his way of looking at the world. But he wasn't anything like that, at bottom he was the calmest, mildest man I've ever known, he wasn't one of God's warriors. If there was any mysticism in his personality, it was a kind of concrete mysticism, firmly anchored in everyday reality.

"We're here, now," he'd always tell me.

He handed me an envelope as we stood on the doorstep. Inside there was a postcard with a picture of mountain pastureland. Above the picture the words "The kingdom of God is within you" were printed in German, and on the back he'd written, *When you sit under the oak tree don't be yourself, be the oak tree, on the grass be the grass, among humans be one of humankind.*

The kingdom of God is within you, remember? I'd already been struck by that phrase during the days when I was living in L'Aquila as an unhappy young bride. In those days, when I'd close my eyes and turn my gaze inward, I couldn't see anything. After I met Father Thomas something changed, I still couldn't see anything, but I wasn't totally blind anymore, a glimmer of light was starting to glow in the darkest depths, every now and then I managed to forget about myself for a few brief instants. It was a weak, tiny light, a faint little flame that wouldn't take much effort to blow out.

The fact that it was there at all, however, made me feel strangely weightless; what I was feeling wasn't happiness, it was joy. There wasn't any euphoria or exaltation, I didn't feel wiser or uplifted. A serene consciousness of existence itself was growing inside me.

Grass on the grass, oak under the oak, one among others.

December 20

PRECEDED BY BUCK, I went up to the attic this morning. How many years ago was the last time I opened that door? There was dust everywhere and giant daddy longlegs hanging from the corners of the beams. In shifting the boxes and cartons around I uncovered two or three nests of dormice, they were sleeping so soundly they didn't notice anything. When you're a child it's fun to go into an attic; it's not so much fun when you're old. Everything that used to be mystery, adventure, discovery, has become a painful memory.

I was looking for the crèche, I had to open several boxes and the two big trunks before I found it.

I came across some of Ilaria's toys and her favorite doll, all wrapped up in newspapers and old rags.

On the bottom I found Augusto's insects, still shiny and perfectly preserved, along with his magnifying glass and other collecting equipment. Nearby there was a caramel tin containing Ernesto's letters, all bound together with a red ribbon. There wasn't anything of yours, you're young and alive, the attic's no place for you as yet.

I opened some of the little packages in one of the trunks and found the few things from my own childhood that had been salvaged from the ruins of our house. They were scorched, blackened, I unwrapped them as though they were relics. Most of them were kitchen objects—an enamel basin, a blue and white china sugar bowl, some silverware, a cake pan, and last of all the loose pages of a coverless book. What book was it? I couldn't remember. It was only when I carefully picked it up and skimmed its opening lines that it all came back to me. I got very emotional, because it wasn't just any old book, it was the book I'd loved the most as a child, the one that used to set my dreams in motion more than any other. It was called *Wonders of the Twenty-first Century*—a science fiction book, in its way. The story was simple but full of imagination. Late in the nineteenth century, two scientists curious to see whether the magnificent oracles of progress would come true have themselves put into a kind of hibernation until the year 2000. After exactly a century, the grandson of a colleague (a scientist in his own right) thaws them out and takes them on an instructive trip around the world aboard a small flying platform. There aren't any extraterrestrials or spaceships in this story, everything that happens in it is solely concerned with man's destiny, the one he's fashioned for himself with his own hands. And, to hear the author tell it, in the intervening hundred years mankind has done a great many things, every one of them marvelous. There's no hunger or poverty in the world anymore, because science, together with technology, has found a way to make every corner of the globe fertile and—more importantly —has seen to it that the fruits of that fertility are distributed equally among all earth's inhabitants.

Many machines have relieved people from the drudgery of work, there's a lot of free time, and so every human being can cultivate the nobler part of his nature, the world resounds on all sides with music, poetry, and serene, learned philosophical discussions. As if that's not enough, the flying platform can transport people from one continent to another in less than an hour. The two old scientists seem quite satisfied: everything their idealistic faith in progress had led them to hypothesize has come true. Leafing through the book, I found my favorite illustration, too: it shows our two corpulent scholars, with Darwinian beards and checkered waistcoats, gazing down in delight from their flying platform.

To dispel any remaining doubt, one of the two dares to ask the question closest to his heart: "What about the anarchists, the revolutionaries? Do they still exist?" "Oh, of course they do," their smiling guide replies. "They live in their very own cities, built under the polar icecaps, so they couldn't hurt other people even if they wanted to."

"And the armies?" the other one is quick to ask. "Why don't we see a single soldier?"

"Armies don't exist anymore," the young man replies.

At this point the two heave a sigh of relief: finally man has returned to his original state of goodness! Their relief is short-lived, however, because their guide goes on to say, "Oh, no, that's not the reason. Man hasn't lost his passion for destruction, he's just learned to restrain himself. Soldiers, cannon, bayonets, all that sort of thing is obsolete. In their place we've got a small but extremely powerful gadget, and it's the reason why there aren't any more wars. All you have to do is climb a mountain and drop this thing from a height, and the whole world will be reduced to a shower of splinters and shreds."

Anarchists! Revolutionaries! A lot of my childhood nightmares sprang from those two words. You might find that a little difficult to understand, but you have to remember that I was seven when the Russian Revolution broke out. I heard grown-ups whispering terrible things to one another, one of my classmates told me the cossacks were about to reach Rome, where they'd water their horses in the sacred fountains. These images horrified my naturally susceptible childish mind: at night, just as I was falling asleep, I could hear the horses' hooves thundering down from the Balkans.

Who could have imagined that I'd live to see quite different horrors, much more shocking than horses galloping through the streets of Rome! When I read that book as a little girl, I did some complicated arithmetic to figure out whether I'd get a glimpse of the year 2000. Ninety seemed a pretty advanced age to me, but not impossible to reach. The whole idea was rather intoxicating, I felt a slight sense of superiority toward all those who wouldn't survive into the twenty-first century.

But now that we're almost there, I know I'll never make it. I don't feel any regret or nostalgia, I'm just very tired, of all those marvels my book promised I've seen only one come true: the tiny, extremely powerful gadget. I don't know if everyone who's coming to the end of his days has this sudden sense of having lived too long, of having seen too much, felt too much. When I think about the span of nearly a century I've lived through, the basic impression I've got is that time has somehow started accelerating. Then again, maybe people who lived in the Stone Age felt the same way about the passing years, I'll never know. A day is still a day, the night is still longer or shorter in proportion to the length of the day, the length of the day depends on the seasons. All that's the same as it was in the Stone Age. The sun rises and sets. Astronomically speaking, if there's a difference it's mighty small.

Yet I've got the feeling that everything's going faster now. The passage of time makes so many things happen, history's always aiming different events at us. You feel more and more tired at the end of each day; at the end of your life, you're exhausted. Just think about the Russian Revolution and communism! I saw its rise, I couldn't sleep at night because of Bolsheviks; I saw it spread into many countries and divide the world into two great wedges, a white one on this side and a black one on that—black and white in perpetual conflict with each other—and that conflict made us all hold our breath: there was the gadget, it had already fallen once, and it could fall again at any moment. Then, suddenly, on a day like any other, I turn on the TV and discover that all this is over, they're tearing down walls and barbed-wire fences and statues: the great utopia of the century became a dinosaur in less than a month. Now it's embalmed, it stands harmless and immobile in the middle of a hall, and everyone files past it and says, How big it was, oh, how it was terrible!

I was talking about communism, but I could have been talking about anything else, so much has passed in front of my eyes and nothing's left of any of it. Do you see now why I say that time has started going faster? What could happen in the course of a single lifetime during the Stone Age? The season of rain, then snow, the season of sun accompanied by locust invasions, a few bloody skirmishes with nasty neighbors, perhaps a small meteorite might crash to earth and leave behind a smoking crater. Beyond your own field, or on the other side of the river, nothing else existed; since the extent of the world was unknown, time necessarily moved more slowly.

The Chinese are supposed to say, "May you live in interesting times." Is this a benevolent hope, a way of wishing you well? I don't think so, it doesn't sound that auspicious to me, it sounds like a curse. Interesting times are troubled times, when lots of things happen. I've lived through very interesting times, but maybe the ones you live in will be even more interesting. The turn of the millennium may be nothing but an astronomical convention, but it always seems to bring some great earth-shattering event.

On January 1, 2000, the birds in the trees will wake up at the same time as they did on December 31, 1999; they'll sing in the same way, and as soon as they've finished singing they'll start hunting for food: a day just like the day before. For humans, though, everything will be different. Maybe—if the great chastisement that some are expecting fails to arrive—people will apply themselves with good-will to the construction of a better world. Will it be like this? Maybe, but then again maybe not. The signals I've been able to make out are all different and contradictory. One day it seems to me that man's just a great monkey in thrall to his instincts and unfortunately capable of manipulating sophisticated, extremely dangerous machines; but the next day I have the impression that the worst is over and the nobler aspects of the human spirit are finally beginning to gain the upper hand. Which hypothesis is correct? Who can say, maybe neither one, maybe what will really happen on the first night of the twenty-first century is that Heaven, in order to punish man for his stupidity and the foolish waste of his potential, will send upon the earth a terrible rain of fire and brimstone.

In the year 2000 you'll be barely twenty-four years old and you'll see whatever happens, but I'll have already passed on, carrying my unsatisfied

December 20

curiosity with me to the grave. Will you be ready, will you be prepared to deal with the new times? If a fairy should come down from the sky right now and tell me to make three wishes, do you know what I'd ask for? I'd ask her to change me into a dormouse, a little bird, a house spider, something that can live close to you without being seen. I don't know what your future holds, I can't even imagine it, but since I love you, this not knowing makes me suffer. The few times we talked about your future it didn't seem at all rosy to you: with the absolute conviction of adolescence, you believed that the unhappiness tormenting you then would torment you forever. I'm convinced of the exact opposite. But why, you'll wonder, what can have put such a crazy notion in my head? Just Buck, sweetheart, it's always been just Buck. Because when you picked him out at that shelter you thought you'd only picked out a dog from among other dogs. But in reality during those three days you'd been fighting a much more important, much more decisive battle inside yourself: the voice of appearances was appealing to you on one side, the voice of the heart on the other, and without any doubt, without any hesitation, you chose the heart.

At your age then I most probably would have picked a silky, elegant dog, the most prestigious and scented one I could find, a dog I'd take on walks so that people would envy me. My insecurities, the environment I'd been brought up in, had already consigned me to the tyranny of external appearances.

December 21

AFTER HOURS of rummaging around in the attic yesterday, the only things I wound up bringing downstairs were the crèche and the cake pan that survived the bombing. All right for the crèche, you'll say, it's Christmas time, but what about the cake pan? This pan belonged to my grandmother—your great-great-grandmother—and it's the only object we have left to show for all the female side of our family history. Its long stay in the attic had left it pretty rusty, so I carried it straight to the kitchen, put it in the sink, and tried to clean it, using my good hand and the requisite soap pads. Think how many times in its existence it's gone in and out of the oven, how many different (yet similar) hands have filled it with batter. I've brought it down so it can live again, so you can use it and maybe leave it to your own daughters when the time comes, because the history of this humble object sums up and reflects the history of our family's generations.

The moment I saw it at the bottom of the trunk I remembered the last good time we had together. When was it? A year ago, perhaps a little more. Early in the afternoon you came into my room without knocking. I was resting on the bed with my hands folded on my chest, and when you saw me you burst into helpless tears. Your sobs woke me. "What's the matter?" I asked as I sat up. "What's happened?" "It's because you're going to die soon," you answered, crying harder than before. "Goodness," I said, laughing, "let's hope it won't be so soon as all that." Then I added, "You know what? I'll teach you something I know how to do and you don't. That way, when I'm not around anymore you can do it and remember me." I got up and you threw your arms around my neck. My emotions were starting to get the better of me, too, so to calm things down I said, "Well, what shall I teach you to do?" You dried your tears and thought it over for a while, and then you said, "A cake." So we went into the kitchen and commenced a long battle. First of all, you didn't want to put on an apron. You said, "If I put that on I'll have to wear curlers and slippers, too. *Heinous!*" Then when you had to beat the egg whites you came down with a sore wrist, and then you got angry because the butter wouldn't blend with the egg yolks and the oven wasn't ever hot enough. When I licked the wooden spoon I was stirring the chocolate with, I got a brown spot on my nose. You looked at me and burst out laughing. "At your age!" you said. "Aren't you embarrassed? You've got a brown nose like a dog!"

Making that simple cake took an entire afternoon and left the kitchen in a pitiful state. All of a sudden everything was light and easy between us, we were a pair of happy accomplices. It was only after we had finally put the cake in the oven, while you were watching it brown through the glass door, that you suddenly remembered why we had made it and started crying again. I tried to console you as we stood by the oven. "Don't cry," I told you. "It's true that I'll pass away before you do, but even when I'm not here anymore I'll still be here, I'll live in you and your happy memories. You'll see the trees, the vegetables, the flowers, and you'll think about all the great times we had together. The same thing will happen if you sit in my armchair; and if you make the cake I taught you to make today you'll see me there in front of you with chocolate on my nose."

December 22

AFTER BREAKFAST today I went into the living room and started setting up the crèche in its usual spot near the fireplace. First I spread out the green paper, then I arranged the little clumps of dried moss, the palm trees, the stable with Joseph, Mary, the ox, and the ass inside, and scattered around it the various shepherds, goose girls, musicians, pigs, fishermen, hens and roosters, sheep and goats. I used adhesive tape to suspend the blue paper sky over the scene; I put the star of Bethlehem in the right pocket of my dressing gown, and the three kings in the left; then I crossed the room and hung the star on the sideboard, and under-

201

neath, a little distance away, I lined up the kings riding on their camels in single file.

Do you remember? When you were little, with the furious logic that small children have, you'd throw a fit if the star and the three kings were near the crèche right from the start. They had to begin far away and move closer gradually, the star slightly ahead and the kings just behind it. In the same way, you couldn't stand it if Baby Jesus appeared in the manger before his time, and so we had him glide down into the stable at the stroke of midnight on December 24. While I was distributing the sheep on their little green mat, I remembered another thing you used to love to do with the crèche, a game you invented yourself and never got tired of playing. I think Easter gave you the initial idea, because at Easter I used to hide your colored eggs in the garden. At Christmas you'd hide little sheep instead of eggs: when I wasn't looking you'd take one of the flock and put it in the most unlikely place, then you'd come to where I was and start bleating desperately. And then the search would begin, I'd stop whatever I was doing and go through the house saying, "Where are you, little lost sheep? Help me find you, I'll take care of you, you'll be safe." You'd follow me around the whole while, laughing and bleating.

And now, little sheep, where are you? You're

over there among the coyotes and the cactus as I write; when you read this you'll most probably be here, and my things will already be in the attic. Will my words take you to a safe place? I'm not presumptuous enough to believe that, perhaps they'll only get on your nerves, they'll confirm the low opinion you had of me before you left. Maybe you'll only be able to understand me when you're older; you'll be able to understand me after you've traveled that mysterious road that leads from intransigence to compassion.

Compassion, I said, not pity. If you pity me, I'm going to come back like some wicked little spirit and play a bunch of nasty tricks on you. I'll do the same thing if you're falsely modest instead of truly humble, or if you get carried away with brainless chatter instead of remaining silent. Light bulbs will explode, plates will fly off shelves, your underwear will wind up draped over lampshades, I won't give you a moment's rest from dawn until deep into the night.

But it's not true, I won't do anything. If I'm around somewhere, if I can see you somehow, I'll just be sad, the way I'm sad every time I see a life thrown away, a life that hasn't been able to make the journey all the way to love. Take care of yourself. As you grow up, you'll often get the urge to change things, to right wrongs, but every time you do, remember that the first revolution, the first and the most important, has to take place within yourself. Fighting for an idea without having an idea of yourself is one of the most dangerous things you can do.

Every time you feel lost, confused, think about trees, remember how they grow. Remember that a tree with lots of branches and few roots will get toppled by the first strong wind, while the sap hardly moves in a tree with many roots and few branches. Roots and branches must grow in equal measure, you have to stand both inside of things and above them, because only then will you be able to offer shade and shelter, only then will you be able to cover yourself with leaves and fruit at the proper season.

And later on, when so many roads open up before you, you don't know which to take, don't pick one at random; sit down and wait. Breathe deeply, trustingly, the way you breathed on the day when you came into the world, don't let anything distract you, wait and wait some more. Stay still, be quiet, and listen to your heart. Then, when it speaks, get up and go where it takes you.